STRIKER

SENTINEL SECURITY #3

ANNA HACKETT

Striker

Published by Anna Hackett

Copyright 2022 by Anna Hackett

Cover by Mayhem Cover Creations

Cover image by Wander Aguiar

Edits by Tanya Saari

ISBN (ebook): 978-1-922414-72-4

ISBN (paperback): 978-1-922414-73-1

Heart of Eon - Romantic Book of the Year (Ruby) winner 2020

Cyborg - PRISM Award Winner 2019

Edge of Eon and Mission: Her Protection - Romantic Book of the Year (Ruby) finalists 2019

Unfathomed and Unmapped - Romantic Book of the Year (Ruby) finalists 2018

Unexplored – Romantic Book of the Year (Ruby) Novella Winner 2017

Return to Dark Earth – One of Library Journal's Best E-Original Books for 2015 and two-time SFR Galaxy Awards winner

At Star's End – One of Library Journal's Best E-Original Romances for 2014

The Phoenix Adventures – SFR Galaxy Award Winner for Most Fun New Series and "Why Isn't This a Movie?" Series

Beneath a Trojan Moon – SFR Galaxy Award Winner and RWAus Ella Award Winner

Hell Squad – SFR Galaxy Award for best Post-Apocalypse for Readers who don't like Post-Apocalypse

Sign up for my VIP mailing list and get your *free box set* containing three action-packed romances.

Visit here to get started: www.annahackett.com

CHAPTER ONE

Trouble was coming.

Hadley Lockwood sipped her champagne and scanned the swanky party. It was being held in a restaurant in the Shard. She had to admit that she loved the modern skyscraper, and the way it contrasted with the old, historic charm of London. And the view of the Thames and city from here was first class. She eyed Tower Bridge for a second, before she looked back at the guests.

She spotted several members of Parliament, some high-ranking government officials, and the chief of the Secret Intelligence Service, known to most as MI6.

Her old boss.

Yes, trouble here would be bad. Most of these people were in their off mode, and not expecting problems.

Hadley sighed. She'd just wanted a simple evening—attend the party, go home for a cup of tea, and read a book. But no, some bad guy had to ruin it.

She sipped again. There was no point in wasting good champagne. She really liked Dom Pérignon.

Unfortunately, she couldn't truly enjoy the champers the way she'd like to with her finely tuned radar for trouble pinging. Loudly. Her years at MI6 had developed it, honed it. She looked around again at so many of London's VIPs, but couldn't tell who was setting it off.

She spotted her current boss talking with some officials from MI6. He stood out, and was very easy to look at.

Killian "Steel" Hawke's sharp, handsome face was impassive, but after working for him for over a year, she could read him quite well. He wasn't loving the hobnobbing, but he knew it was a necessary evil when you worked in private security. They'd flown in that morning on the company jet—one perk of working for Sentinel Security was all the toys. Killian kept his security team well-stocked, and well-compensated.

Another perk was living in New York. Hadley loved the vibrant city, and didn't miss gray, old London much.

Killian met her gaze across the crowd. He didn't react, but she knew he'd come her way soon. She did a little loop of the room—smiling at people she knew, and air kissing a few old acquaintances.

"Ravishing as always, Hadley," an old contact from MI6 said.

"You too, darling," Hadley replied.

"Hadley, you get more beautiful every time I see you," an old friend of her father's rasped.

She laughed. "You're such a charmer, Sir James."

She finally found a quiet spot by the floor-to-ceiling

windows. All the small talk and compliments left her cold. Finally, the reflection in the glass showed her that Killian was heading her way.

Gosh, he was a handsome devil. It was a shame he was both her boss, and a friend. And there was none of that kind of chemistry between them.

She liked and respected Killian. A lot. He'd offered her a job that she loved, and given her a found family that had filled a tired, jaded hole inside of her she hadn't known she'd had.

They'd bumped into each other a few times when she'd been at MI6, and he'd been with the CIA. Steel was a bit of a legend.

But she also knew he was a man who often pushed himself too hard, especially when it came to protecting his people.

"You look gorgeous as always." Killian stopped beside her. "Blue is your color."

She swished the skirt of her royal-blue dress. She wore a long skirt in deference to London's cool weather, but the neckline plunged deep in front. She had no qualms about utilizing all her assets.

"I spoke with the Minister for Energy and Climate earlier. He talked to my cleavage."

Killian's teeth flashed. "The poor guy's about a hundred and four. You probably made his night."

She turned to face him. "Killian, something's wrong. I can feel it."

Now, her boss turned to look at her, his face settling into serious lines. "Security for this party is tight."

"We both know that's not always enough. There are some high-powered people here."

"The trouble can't be for us," he said. "I made sure our names were not on the guest list."

Hadley shrugged. "There are lots of juicy targets." Including some of her family. She turned and caught sight of her parents.

Lord Charles Lockwood, Baron Astley, and Lady Caroline Lockwood. They looked as they always did—posh, rich, and aloof. She'd already said hello to them, and kept it mercilessly short.

She didn't always like them, but they were her parents, and she cared about them. If something went down tonight, she didn't want to see them hurt.

Killian gave a sharp nod. "I'll look around."

Her shoulders relaxed a little. "Thanks, Kill."

He squeezed her arm. "Ready for the meeting tomorrow?"

She nodded. It was the reason they were here, instead of back in the huge warehouse in New York that Killian had converted into the Sentinel Security headquarters. They had a meeting with MI6 about a classified project. Killian hadn't told her anything.

"I'm always ready," she said.

"So you are. Keep an eye out." He stalked off, cutting through the party crowd like a knife. Several women looked at him, then cast Hadley envious looks.

"There you are," a cultured voice said. "*Please* tell me you're shagging him and it's amazing."

Hadley's older sister Annabelle sidled up to her, wearing a classy Stella McCartney dress.

"He's my boss," Hadley said.

"So? He is *fine*." Annabelle smiled. "How are you, darling? Still off saving the world?"

"My little corner of it."

Annabelle rolled her eyes. She had their father's brown eyes, while Hadley had their mother's light-blue shade.

"It sounds so tedious," Annabelle said. "You should come home, enjoy the good life."

Annabelle's idea of the good life was attending parties like this, shopping, ensuring the kids were with the nanny, and the odd ski trip to France. She'd married a wealthy London businessman, and had a very cool, British marriage. They both cheated, but did it discreetly, and neither of them cared.

All so icily civilized.

Hadley knew that was life. Real love was a crapshoot. Oh, it happened, of course. Two of her fellow Sentinel Security friends, Nick and Matteo—men she cared for deeply—had recently fallen in love with two wonderful women. Hell, they'd charged into it.

Thankfully, Hadley loved Lainie and Gabbi. They were both so good for the men.

But those couples were the exception that proved the rule.

Real love required trust, and Hadley had a short supply of that. Her family had been the first to give her lessons in not trusting. She loved them, but she wouldn't trust them as far as she could throw them. They were all selfish to the bone.

Then, at MI6, she'd learned the rest of her lessons. She'd seen many accomplished liars and expert betrayers.

And as a young, idealistic agent, she'd let one idiot fool her. She'd thought she'd been in love, and she'd learned a very hard, almost deadly, lesson.

She sipped her champagne again. Trusting someone was a risk usually not worth taking.

She trusted her fellow Sentinel Security team members, but that was it.

"Come home and stop working so hard," her sister continued.

"Annabelle, have you seen the weather here?" As if to help make Hadley's point, fat raindrops hit the glass. "I'll take New York weather and shopping any day."

Her sister nodded. "Fair point." Then she lowered her voice. "Not to mention some strapping American men to sample."

Hadley hid her eye roll. "How are the kids?"

Annabelle waved a hand. "Oh, you know, noisy."

God, her sister. "Tell them Auntie Hadley says hi. I'll stop by to visit when I can."

"Mummy and Daddy want you to come over for dinner one night."

Hadley groaned, and Annabelle grinned.

That meant a stuffy dinner at their parents' home, along with whatever stuffy single man they tried to foist off on her.

"I'm not sure I'll have the time."

Annabelle snorted. "You know that won't stop them. Bring someone. Maybe your hot boss."

"No. I'm not subjecting Killian to that."

"Someone else, then."

"No." A tingle started at the back of her neck.

It got stronger. She idly hoped it was wrong, for once, but it was never wrong. Trouble was close.

Suddenly, a strong, muscular arm wrapped around her waist in an exceptionally possessive way.

She looked up and her body went stiff. She looked into extraordinary hazel eyes, filled with gold flecks. Eyes she'd never, ever admit that she sometimes dreamed about.

"I'm sorry," the newcomer drawled. "Can I steal her away?"

Annabelle blinked, then grinned. "Sure. Go ahead."

Then, British billionaire Bennett Knightley, whisked Hadley away and onto the dance floor, and she found herself pressed up against a hard, suit-clad body.

THERE WAS nothing quite as attractive as a beautiful woman shooting you an annoyed glare.

Bennett Knightley slid an arm around Hadley's waist. "Ms. Lockwood."

"Mr. Knightley," she clipped.

Oh, there was something else as attractive as the glare —it was the cool, sharp tone as she said his name. She had the rare ability to be polite and tell him he was a dickhead at the same time.

His cock tightened.

Down, boy, or she'll cut you off.

They moved across the dance floor, and of course, she

7

danced as easily as she breathed. He could only dance because his mum had forced all her kids into lessons. Bennett and his two brothers had suffered through theirs, while their sister had laughed at them gleefully.

But he wasn't surprised that Hadley "Striker" Lockwood danced well. As far as he could tell, she did everything well. Hadley was frighteningly competent at everything.

He pulled her closer to avoid bumping into the tipsy, millionaire owner of a high-end department store, and an equally tipsy blonde who looked vaguely familiar. Bennett thought she might host a television morning show.

But as he got more of a feel of Hadley, his thoughts scattered. She was built for temptation. Tall, with curves in all the right places. But as a former special forces soldier, he wasn't fooled. Despite the creamy hint of breasts her dress displayed, and the thick, light-brown hair that was captured in a sleek, elegant style, her body toned. Hadley could use everything at her disposal as a weapon, if required.

It was what had made her a very good MI6 agent.

"What are you doing here?" she asked.

"I was invited. Unfortunately, I get lots of invites to parties like these." Most of which were tedious, filled with people who were mostly interested in talking about themselves.

"The tough life of a multimillionaire," she said.

He smiled at her. "Billionaire."

She rolled her beautiful blue eyes—they were pale, like Arctic ice. "Sorry, *billionaire*. How is business?"

His gut tightened. "Secura is ticking along fine."

"There's always a market for weapons of war."

His brows drew together. "I don't sell weapons. We sell gear. Body armor, uniforms, bedding, meals. Everything else soldiers need in the field. The stuff that often gets neglected or is of poor, cheap quality. It isn't just bullets that takes lives."

He heard the edge to his voice. He knew firsthand that good people got injured or killed because of the damn clothes they wore in the field, or because the gear and food they had was sub-standard.

Hadley cocked her head, studying his face. "You lost someone."

Bennett fought the urge to move his shoulders. Damn her for being too perceptive. The Special Air Service had trained him to stay still when required, and show nothing. He cleared his throat. "I lost lots of people. Many of them for no good reason."

But for a second, he saw the face of Hamed. A good man who used his language skills to help. Bennett had worked and fought alongside him, and he'd saved Bennett's arse too many times to count. Hamed Rahmani had been a man who'd made do with what he had to help his country.

A man who'd died, splattered in blood, on the desert sand of a rundown village.

Not long after Hamed had died, Bennett had left the military. He'd come home, determined to make a difference in other ways.

Secura had been born. His company specialized in high-tech fabrics; lightweight, but durable, gear soldiers needed. Better, more nutritious meals. Hell, he spent a fuck-load on his team of scientists for research and development. And Secura had become more successful than he'd ever dreamed.

As he and Hadley whirled around the dance floor, he spotted Killian Hawke. The man raised his drink, and Bennett nodded.

Now, there was a man not to underestimate, and not to turn your back on. Bennett was damn glad they were on the same side.

"So, you have a meeting at MI6 tomorrow," Bennett said.

Blue eyes flashed. "None of your business."

"Didn't Killian tell you that I'm your backup, if you need help while you're here?"

She shot him a smile. "I don't need help."

"But you don't know what the job is yet."

"It's classified."

"Mmm. It's okay to ask for help, Hadley."

"Not if I don't need it."

Yes, he'd noted her fierce independence before. He'd seen her smile, seen her with her Sentinel Security friends, but under it, he sensed how self-contained she was. Could feel the walls that he suspected could sustain an attack or a stealth invasion.

What had forced her to build them? And what would it take for her to let someone in?

You think you deserve to be that someone? The sly voice in his head made his gut clench.

His gaze moved over her face. "Christ, you're beautiful."

She blinked. Her gaze dropped to his mouth.

"Ah, I finally said something that's made you speechless."

"Hardly." Her gaze flicked back up to his. "It takes more than some clumsy compliment from you, Knightley."

"It's the truth. I love your perfume too." It was a blend of citrus and floral that teased the senses. He shifted his hand a little and touched her wrist, stroked her pulse point.

He felt it beating hard. She wasn't as immune to him as she liked to make out.

But she didn't snap at him, instead, a serious look slipped over her face, and she scanned the crowd.

Bennett's arms tightened. "What's wrong?"

"I've just got a feeling."

He followed her gaze. Nothing looked amiss. "You're sure?"

"Yes. I've been feeling it for a while. Something's off."

"Okay." He studied the partygoers closer.

Her gaze met his. "That's it? You believe me?"

"Hadley, you were scary good in your previous line of work, and I got a firsthand look at how good you are in your current job in Italy."

"Where you butted into a sensitive operation."

"Where I *helped* you get your job done."

She huffed out a breath, but her attention was on the guests. "Can you see anyone who doesn't belong?"

Bennett took a good look around. All the partygoers seemed relaxed, and were enjoying themselves, chatting and laughing. Some looked like they'd had a little too much to drink.

"No." He took a closer look at the servers, and the suited guards standing discreetly by the walls. "There's a lot of security here tonight."

She huffed out another breath, not once missing a step. "Maybe I'm just tired."

"Jet lag is a killer."

"Oh, I don't suffer jet lag. I don't believe in it." Her nose wrinkled. "And I've had plenty of practice in avoiding it." Just then, he felt her stiffen. "Knightley—"

Her tone of voice made him turn his head.

A young man in a rumpled suit staggered onto the dance floor. He was sweating, nervous, his face unnaturally pale, even for the end of winter in London.

Fuck.

"N-nobody move!" The man opened his jacket to show the bomb vest strapped to his chest.

Screams cut across the party. Bennett heard Hadley curse under her breath.

Then he saw her reach into the slit in her dress and pull out a small, black tactical knife.

She opened it with a well-practiced flick, the diamonds at her wrist glinting, then she quickly concealed the knife in the folds of her skirt.

Annnd he was hard again.

Fuck. Get your head in the game, Knightley. Lust after the hot woman after *the dangerous situation is contained.*

Her blue eyes met his—calm, composed, and calculating.

Bennett gave her a small nod and forced his muscles to stay relaxed. Ready to attack the target.

She edged toward the bomber. "Oh, please don't hurt us."

Damn, even he believed that terrified tone.

"Stay back," the young man yelped. "Just listen." He swiped a shaking arm across his forehead, while his other hand clutched a small detonator attached to a cord. "I have to read something." He fumbled in his pocket.

"*Please.*" Hadley did a stellar impression of pure terror. "I don't want to die."

She moved closer, and Bennett moved in behind her.

The bomber looked up and met Bennett's gaze. He blanched. "M-Mr. Knightley, you aren't supposed to be here."

No, it had been a last-minute decision to attend, when he'd heard Killian and Hadley would be here. Bennett realized two concerning things. One, the bomber was wearing a Secura tactical vest. And two, Bennett recognized the young man.

"Archie, put the detonator down," Bennett said calmly. "Let's talk—"

"I can't. They'll hurt her." He let out a sob. "I can't. It's too late."

Bennett studied the detonator. Thankfully, it didn't have a dead man switch.

Hadley moved closer, without looking like she meant to. He needed to keep Archie's attention off her.

"It's going to be fine." Bennett held up a placating hand. "Now, just let me—"

Hadley struck.

She threw the knife, which slammed into the joint between Archie's shoulder and neck.

The young man cried out, dropping the detonator, leaving it swinging by the cord attached to the vest.

Whirling around, Hadley kicked him in the head. Then, Bennett dove, tackling Archie to the floor.

He kept the man pinned as Hadley opened his jacket.

"It's a fake." She shook her head, and met Bennett's gaze, relief in her eyes. "It's not real."

"Security!" Bennett bellowed. "It's a fake, but let's not take any chances. Clear the party out."

Everyone seemed frozen.

"Everyone out, now!" he shouted.

There was a flurry of activity.

Killian appeared beside them, looking unperturbed. "Have you got this under control?"

Hadley nodded.

"I'll deal with security, and call the police."

Bennett lifted his head. His and Hadley's faces were only inches apart.

"You sure know how to liven up the party, Ms. Lockwood," he said. "Nice takedown."

"Thanks. You weren't too bad yourself." She arched a brow at him. "You know this guy?"

Archie was sobbing hard, incoherent.

Bennett blew out a breath. "Yes, unfortunately, I do. He works for Secura."

CHAPTER TWO

The next morning, Hadley slipped into her heels, then grabbed her coat and handbag.

While she loved her apartment in the Sentinel Security warehouse in New York, she sometimes missed her London flat. She'd kept it and occasionally rented it out for short-stay accommodation. She'd kept it mostly so she had a place to stay when she visited, and didn't have to stay with her parents in their stuffy Mayfair mansion.

Her gaze swept over the open-plan kitchen and living area, with lots of white marble, and her own personal touches.

But the decor couldn't compete with the view. The apartment was in a tower at St. George's Wharf, perched right on the Thames. London was laid out before her. She picked out a few landmarks: Vauxhall Bridge down below, the wheel of the London Eye in the distance. Then her gaze fell on to the white-and-green building that housed the SIS Headquarters, more commonly known as MI6. Once her old stomping ground. It almost looked like a temple, and she'd heard the designer had been inspired by Mayan and Aztec temples.

Well, it was only a six-minute walk, but she needed to get moving so she wasn't late for the meeting with Killian and her old boss, David Farrell.

She slipped on her cashmere coat and headed for the elevator.

After a quick walk in the drizzling rain along the gloomy Thames, she passed through security, and found Killian waiting for her.

"Sleep all right after last night's excitement?" He held out a takeout coffee for her.

"You are the best boss in the world." She took it gratefully and sipped. It was her favorite. A caramel latte. "I slept fine."

After giving statements to the police, she and Killian had finally left the party.

Bennett had still been there, trying to work out why his employee had threatened the party with a fake bomb. Unfortunately, the young man had been hysterical, and not making much sense.

She hoped Knightley had gotten it sorted. She took another sip of coffee. Bennett Knightley was a man who could take care of himself. He didn't need her worrying about him.

The man was rich and powerful. She knew from experience men like that could make their problems disappear. Her father was a master at it.

Still, Knightley wore the devil-may-care, billionaire persona well, but his tough, rangy body didn't hide what he was—a warrior. He was all muscle, and there was a touch of rough around the edges of his tailored suits. He didn't even wear an expensive watch. He wore a simple, battered smartwatch. You could take the man out of the Army, but you couldn't take the Army out of the man.

She worked with an entire team of badasses, and Killian was the king of them. He was a man who was always assessing, always ready for a threat, always ready for a fight.

Bennett Knightley was exactly the same. He'd had her back last night, been one step behind her.

It just added to the attractive package.

So the guy had a rugged face, strong jaw, and piercing hazel eyes. She took another hurried sip of her latte. She could see the attraction, she wasn't blind. But that was it.

Okay, fine. She was reluctantly attracted to him. Any woman would be. But she didn't act on every attraction she felt.

Sex was sex. Relationships were a dangerous minefield. Getting into something with a man required trust, and she found that most men were not worthy of hers. The foreign agent who'd fooled her, then betrayed her, hadn't been. God, she'd been naïve.

The only people she excluded from that were Killian and her workmates. Unfortunately, she didn't feel a burning urge to shag any of them.

But you'd do a certain billionaire in a heartbeat, a tiny voice in her head whispered.

She almost missed a step.

"Okay?" Killian asked.

She cleared her throat. "Yes. Wearing high heels is a hazard you'll never have to worry about."

"Thank fuck."

They walked down the hall to a familiar door. How many times had she walked into her old boss' office? With new intel, before a mission, to get permission for surveillance, or to hand in a report.

"Miss it?"

She glanced at Killian. "No, I don't." She loved Sentinel Security, and she'd needed to change. "You?"

He'd been a legend at the CIA. Hell, in the entire international intelligence community. Killian "Steel" Hawke was a name that put terror in the eyes of some people.

"No." He knocked on the door briskly.

"Come," a voice called out.

David's office was brightly lit, no thanks to the murky gloom outside. She smiled at her old boss. He was a neat, trim man in his fifties, with a silver beard. But all her attention went to the man in the bespoke suit—which she knew at a glance came from Savile Row tailors, Gieves & Hawkes, if she wasn't mistaken—slouched in a guest chair.

What the hell was Bennett Knightley doing here?

"Mr. Knightley," she said.

"Ms. Lockwood."

Even though he looked tired, he radiated a sense of assurance and power that was seductive. He looked like a man who could weather any storm. A woman could lay her head on his broad shoulder, and she'd know he'd protect her.

Hadley mentally shook her head. Mother nature had given men broad shoulders to fool women into trusting them. She was sure it was to ensure the continuation of the human race.

She wasn't so easily fooled anymore.

She noted that Bennett had grooves bracketing his mouth. She guessed he'd had a long night.

"Sit, Hadley. You too, Killian." David dropped into his desk chair, and it squeaked. It was as old as the hills, but he loved it and refused to replace it. Duct tape patches added an extra bit of flair.

"Why is Mr. Knightley here?" Hadley slipped her coat off.

She saw Bennett's gaze drift down her long, fitted skirt. Appreciation shone in his eyes before he glanced away.

Little embers of heat ignited in her belly. *Oh, no.* She sat and crossed her legs.

"Because he's involved in this case," David said.

"The man with the fake bomb at the party is a part of this?" Hadley asked.

A muscle ticked in Bennett's jaw.

"We suspect so." David sighed. "I brought you in, Hadley, because it involves L'Orage."

She stiffened. L'Orage, the storm in French, was a code name for a dangerous arms dealer who, for decades, had supplied most of the world's hotspots. She'd tracked him mercilessly for years. Had watched a good friend pay the price for that pursuit with her life. Hadley had vowed to bring him to justice.

Then he'd disappeared two years ago.

"He's back?" she asked.

David nodded. "Yes."

"And it appears he's targeting my company," Bennett growled.

BENNETT SHOVED down his welling anger.

He wanted to find this L'Orage, and rip the man's head off.

The bastard was targeting Secura. Stopping Secura gear getting to where it was most needed.

That meant people would die.

Bennett would throw all his resources at stopping this arsehole.

He dragged in a breath, finding his calm. He knew that to get the job done, he needed to control his emotions and focus. In the SAS, he'd been damn good at it.

Focusing on Hadley helped him get a lock on it.

Damn, the distraction of slim curves clad in a fitted, dark-gray skirt, and a formfitting, pale-gray top helped a lot. Her hair was loose, and diamonds winked in her ears. He noted that her hair was damp from the rain. She needed an umbrella.

The sexy executive look gave him plenty of X-rated ideas.

If she knew what he was thinking, she'd do him bodily harm.

He studied her profile—slim nose, delicate jaw line, perfectly shaped ears. The beautiful features hid a will of pure steel.

"Why don't you start at the beginning?" Killian suggested.

"Secura had a shipment of bulletproof vests go missing six months ago," Bennett said. "It's not uncommon. Logistics get screwed up sometimes. We couldn't find it. Then, soon after, a shipment of high-tech fabric uniforms was stolen from a warehouse, en route to a customer."

"We got wind that the gear was spotted in the hands of terrorists and rebel groups in Africa," David said.

"It's not weapons, but my company spends a lot of time and money on R&D," Bennett said. "Our gear is the best there is, and it helps save lives."

"And this gear will make it that much harder to stop the terrorists and rebels," Hadley said. "L'Orage has a history of stealing weapons from military or police locations, and selling them for a tidy profit."

"And now it seems he's branched out into body armor and other supplies," Bennett said, flexing his hand.

"He's well-connected," she said. "He has a long list of clients. He has contacts in the right places to get shipping schedules and security details, and more. He's bribed people on the inside when he can."

Bennett kept his face impassive. The bastard sure had info on Secura that he shouldn't have.

"And the would-be bomber at last night's party?" Killian asked. "He was one of yours?"

Bennett felt a muscle tick in his jaw. "Yes, Archie Martin. He's an employee at Secura. He was carrying a note. It was the usual rhetoric about stopping sending our soldiers to die on foreign soil. Stop interfering with other countries."

"Had Martin shown support for this sort of thing before?" Killian asked.

"No. He's former military himself, worked as a communications and information systems specialist in the British Navy. He's a good employee." Bennett scraped a hand through his hair. He'd seen Archie breakdown last night. Something had happened to him. Something had forced him into this.

"Was he your leak?" Hadley asked. "Could he be involved with L'Orage?"

"Possibly," Bennett replied.

"We're holding Mr. Martin for questioning," David said. "But he's had an episode and is under medical supervision. We can't get any useful information out of him."

Bennett's gut tightened. Whatever had happened, Archie was still one of his. He'd ensure the young man got the help—medical and legal—that he needed. "As far as I can tell, I don't believe Archie had access to all our shipment details."

Hadley's mouth tightened. "So you might have more than one leak at Secura?"

Now his hand balled into a fist. "I plan to find out." He already had his security team scouring Archie's computer and company phone.

"This has L'Orage stamped all over it." She crossed her legs to the other side. "He has tentacles everywhere. I'd hoped he was gone."

"I suspect you were getting too close," David said.

Killian nodded. "He was feeling the heat, and went underground for a bit."

"Well, he's back now, and I want him stopped." Bennett would do whatever he had to in order to achieve that. Secura and the work they did was too important to him.

He saw Hadley eyeing him with a narrowed gaze.

"So, you need to find your mole," Hadley said. "Or moles."

"I'll find them."

"They're not going to just announce themselves to you," she said.

"No, they're not." David leaned back in his chair. "We have an interest in helping Knightley with his problem."

"Why?" Killian asked.

"Because Secura has several classified projects in the works with MI6," David said.

Hadley leaned forward, her gaze sharpening on Bennett. "You're going into arms?"

"No." God, she was so distrusting. "Our primary project with MI6 is a high-tech, lightweight exosuit for soldiers and agents to use in the field. To increase strength and stamina."

Hadley's eyes widened. "You're close to a workable, light exosuit?"

"Yes. Another project is bullet-resistant fabric for uniforms."

Killian raised a brow. "That's something I'd be interested in."

"And I'm guessing L'Orage and every criminal organization he supplies, as well," David said dryly. "Hadley, I asked you here because of your knowledge of L'Orage.

So I'm paying Steel here a hefty sum for you. I want you to help Knightley find his mole, and then take down L'Orage."

Hadley straightened.

"And I believe the best way to do that is for you to go undercover at Secura," David added.

Bennett stiffened. Have the temptation of Hadley Lockwood in his office, every day?

Shit.

"Sir, do you really think that's necessary?" she asked.

"I think it's an excellent idea," Killian said. "You need to be up close and personal. You'll find Knightley's mole quicker that way."

She turned her head and met Bennett's gaze. He pressed his lips together. They had to do this. Whatever was necessary.

"You have my full support," Bennett said.

Hadley gave a reluctant nod. "Very well."

"Ferret L'Orage out," David said. "I do not want our top-secret projects falling into terrorist hands."

Bennett nodded and stood. "Ms. Lockwood, a moment? We can discuss your cover at Secura."

She rose with liquid elegance. He followed her out of the office and tried not to look at the way her skirt hugged her ass.

She led him to a glass-walled conference room.

"I'm not sure this is a good plan," she said.

He forced a smile. "Think you'll have trouble keeping your hands off me, if you see me daily?"

She shot him a withering look. "Won't your staff get suspicious if I just turn up?"

"I have an opening for a new head of communications. We've been looking for a while, and you can pull anything off, so no, they won't get suspicious."

She hitched a hip up on the conference room table. "Okay. We have to find L'Orage. We can't fail."

"I don't fail." He kept his tone firm, implacable. "This bastard has targeted my company. He's stopping my shipments and gear getting to the people who need it. He targeted one of my employees." He lowered his voice. "It pisses me off."

She tilted her head. "This sounds like a crusade."

"No one fucks with me or mine." He moved closer to her. "And now, that includes you." He drew in a deep breath, drawing in her scent.

Something sparked in her eyes. "I'm perfectly capable of taking care of myself, Mr. Knightley. I have no use for overbearing, overprotective alpha males."

"You'll have to find a use." He made himself step back and drag in a breath. "I'll email you details for your cover job. You'll need an assumed name."

"Yes. It's best to keep it as close as we can to my real name. I have an old alias I can use. Halle Atwood."

"Good. Then I'll see you tomorrow morning, Ms. Atwood." Bennett turned to leave.

"Knightley?"

He glanced back.

"We will find him," she said.

He gave her a decisive nod. "We will."

CHAPTER THREE

"And so, I'm going undercover at Secura as the new head of communications." Hadley dusted on some eyeshadow.

"Undercover with a sexy billionaire. Tough gig, Hadley."

She heard the amusement in her friend Hex's voice. She glanced at the tablet propped up on the vanity in her bathroom.

It was early in New York, but Jet "Hex" Adler kept crazy hours. She was Sentinel Security's tech wizard, and a former CIA hacker, who could make any computer dance to her tune.

On-screen, Hex was sipping coffee from a huge mug.

"As long as the billionaire doesn't get in my way, I'll be fine."

Hex made a sound. "You should let him get in your way, girl. Let that Grade-A, gorgeous man get his hands on you."

"I'm working."

"You're always working, and I'm your friend. I know you don't like letting anyone too close. Especially men."

Hadley looked away, selected a lipstick, and ruthlessly concentrated on applying it. "He's a rich, entitled man dedicated to his company. I know men like that. Selfish ones who go after what they want and damn the consequences."

"Hadley, he's not your parents and he isn't Casper the Rat," Hex said.

The name still hit like an arrow. Piercing, hurting, generating a strange mélange of emotions: rage, regret, embarrassment.

"I don't let foolish mistakes rule my life."

Hex was quiet for a second. "Yes, you do."

"Jet..."

Her friend leaned closer to the screen. "He played you. You trusted him, fell for him, and he was a foreign agent. I get how that must've felt, but Bennett Knightley is not Casper Abbott aka Casper Ahmadi. You can trust Knightley, or at least give him a chance."

Hadley looked at her reflection in the mirror. No man was worth the risk. She never again wanted to feel how she'd felt when she'd uncovered the truth about Casper.

That he'd played her for months, led her on, all to steal her password to try and access the MI6 system.

Hadley had stopped him, but his betrayal had shattered something inside her.

"I have no personal interest in Bennett Knightley."

On-screen, Hex rolled her eyes. They were unique: one was blue and one was green. "Liar."

"I'm here to get the job done. I warned everyone that Knightley can't be fully trusted."

Hex frowned. "You think he's involved with L'Orage?"

"No, but he's driven by his own agenda. The man left the Army and became a billionaire making equipment for the military. Something deep is driving him, and I think he'll take down anything or anyone standing in his way. That makes him dangerous." It also made him a bad bet for any sort of intimate relationship. She didn't think he'd make room for a woman in the long term.

"Or it makes him a good guy, Hadley," Hex insisted.

"No one's all good."

With a harrumph, Hex sipped her coffee. "Paranoia does not look good on you." She tapped on her keyboard. "Do you know that most of Secura's employees were former military, or are the family of military members?"

Hadley stilled. "Are you running searches on Knightley?"

"Not the full shebang. Just a little nosing." Hex made a humming sound. "Some of his employees were having trouble getting work anywhere due to PTSD or other injuries."

Hadley looked into the mirror, mind whirling. She tried to make sense of this revelation. Who the hell was Bennett Knightley?

A big, broad-shouldered man stomped by behind Hex without saying hello. Hadley arched a brow. "Bram looks extra cheery today."

Hex pulled a face. "He's taking grumpy to new levels."

Bram "Excalibur" O'Donovan was another key member of the Sentinel Security team. He was tall, big, with sexy, dark-red hair, and the temperament of a grump. He did his best to avoid people.

He was former special forces with the Irish Defense Forces, the Army Ranger Wing, and had also done a stint in Ireland's Military Intelligence. He was an invaluable member of the Sentinel Security team. The man was very handy in a fight.

Hex lowered her voice. "I think it's a woman."

Hadley blinked. "Bram and a woman?"

Her friend nodded. "I think he was seeing someone, and maybe she broke it off. He hasn't said anything, so I'm trying to read between the lines. Or grunts and scowls."

Hadley knew Bram's MO with women. The man was less trusting than she was. Casual, one-night hookups were his thing. No strings, no promises, no repeats.

"You're sure?" Hadley asked.

"No," Hex said. "Trying to decode his grunts is tough, so I'm not sure. Anyway, I think Killian wants Bram to head your way to help. So you can have a try at working out what's wrong with him."

Hadley looked at her watch. She had no time to solve Bram's problems today. "I have to run. A car is picking me up soon."

"Good luck with your first day on the new job with the hot billionaire."

Hadley rolled her eyes. "I'll keep you posted. What are Killian's movements today?"

"He has about a million meetings to attend." Hex

laughed. "You can imagine how thrilled that makes him. He's catching up with some existing London-based clients, and he has several more meetings planned with new ones over the next few days. He's on call if you need him."

The boogeyman of the intelligence world, Steel, having to play the businessman. It made Hadley smile.

Then she looked back at her friend. "Hex, I have a favor to ask."

Hex's face turned serious. "Anything."

"Nightingale House. There's a mother and daughter there at the moment who—"

The hacker smiled. "Already taken care of. Gabbi is going to pop in there a few times while you're gone. We know how much time you spend down there."

Relief hit Hadley. Hex had come with her numerous times to the domestic violence shelter. Sentinel Security had been approached to talk to the women on self-defense, and Killian had volunteered Hadley. She'd been so touched by the women and children, all escaping desperate, dangerous situations, that she'd continued to visit.

She'd felt a sense of kinship. These women had been betrayed by the men closest to them.

"Thanks. Um, tell Gabbi the little girl, Cora, likes cupcakes with pink icing."

Hex's smile widened. "I'll tell her. God, you're a softie."

"I am not. Now, I have to go. I might need your help on this case later."

"You know where to find me."

Hadley waved. Once the screen went blank, she checked her reflection. Her navy-blue dress fit like a glove. It had a high neckline, and was sleeveless, and she thought it was classy, with an edge of sexy.

Not that she was wearing it for Bennett Knightley.

Shaking her head, she grabbed her tablet, then her camel-colored coat. She shoved the tablet in her large handbag, then slipped on her nude heels.

She was ready.

The car was waiting for her outside. Thankfully, it wasn't a long drive to Wimpole Street in the West End, where Secura's head office was located.

She climbed out, taking in the lovely, renovated 1920s building. She knew it was situated over a disused underground station, and spanned four levels.

She liked it. In the lobby, she found a funky vibe with brick walls and pops of color. One wall held framed photographs of soldiers from all around the world. Her gaze zoomed in on one showing the silhouette of a muscular soldier, cradling an assault rifle, and patting the head of a tough-looking military dog. Even though his face was looking away, she knew instantly that it was Bennett.

She checked in with Secura security. She was happy to see they looked competent, and had good procedures.

Soon, she had a new ID badge. As she headed for the elevator, a familiar form pushed away from the wall.

"Is this the secret to making billions?" she asked. "Leaning against walls?"

"Funny," Bennett said.

Today he wore dark-gray suit pants, and a white shirt.

He had no jacket, and his sleeves were rolled up to show powerful forearms covered in a smattering of brown hair.

Heat stirred in Hadley's belly, and she blew out a breath. Damn, she was a sucker for a man in a suit, but rolled-up sleeves... They were like a flame to dry tinder.

Get it under control, Hadley. They're just arms. He's just a man.

Men and sex were *not* important. They were just distractions, and she had a job to do.

Bennett held out a takeout coffee cup.

"What's this?" she asked.

"Poison." His face was deadpan.

She took a little sip and the delicious coffee flavor hit her. "How did you know I like caramel lattes?"

He winked. "That's classified." He led her into an elevator.

Hadley sipped again, trying to suppress the little flutter in her belly.

"I'll introduce you to key staff members," he said. "We have to attend some meetings—"

"I can be convincing, Knightley."

He eyed her. "I have no doubt. I'll schedule a couple of one-on-one sessions in my office. Ostensibly to talk about your new job."

"But really?"

"I have Archie's laptop and phone for us to look at."

Hadley smiled. "Excellent."

"I want L'Orage found, Hadley. I won't let him destroy my company and steal my gear."

She heard anger in his voice, along with pure steel. He meant every word.

"Then let's get to work," she said.

———

BENNETT WATCHED Hadley charm all his senior managers. She played the part of smart, experienced Halle Atwood very well. She rarely poured that charm on him. In fact, she most often eyed him with suspicion.

A faint smile crossed his face. He got to see the real Hadley Lockwood, not the carefully curated façade.

She sure was something. A very tempting something.

The dress she wore clung to her curves. When she leaned over to look at something on his CFO's computer, Bennett's gaze dropped to her arse.

He stifled a groan. Never, not once, had he lusted after anyone in the office. He wasn't a man to indulge his fantasies during work hours, especially not when that work was so important to him. But Hadley was stirring up his imagination.

Shit.

"Thank you." Hadley smiled at Peter. "I look forward to learning more about Secura from you."

Peter flushed a little. He was fifty-five, divorced, and he wasn't exactly smooth around the ladies. Bennett knew a bunch of the twenty-something assistants were trying to get poor Peter into online dating.

"Cheers, Peter. I need to steal Halle away now." Bennett took her arm. "We have a lot to discuss."

Her blue eyes met his. "Sure thing, boss."

Shit. His cock twitched.

He crossed the office, quickly introducing her to a

few more people in some of the open-plan areas.

Then his assistant Maudie popped up from her desk. She had a cloud of short, curly, blonde hair, English Rose skin, and wore one of her usual vintage outfits—this one was a black skirt with some flare, and a stripy blouse, topped with a huge flower brooch.

"Good morning, Maudie," he said.

His assistant shot him a grumpy look, then glared at Hadley. "This is the new manager?"

Hadley blinked at Maudie's less-than-welcoming tone.

"Halle, this is my assistant, Maudie. She keeps us in line around here, and mostly, she charms us with her upbeat cheer and pleasant demeanor."

That earned him another withering glance.

"Okay, just kidding. While she may not have a sunny personality, she's a damn good assistant," he said.

"Then I guess it's nice to meet you, Maudie." Hadley smiled. "I like your outfit."

Maudie rolled her eyes. "I can tell designer when I see it." Her gaze ran over Hadley's dress. "I don't think you're into anything vintage."

Hadley rolled her shoulder. "I have some vintage Chanel."

Maudie just made an impatient sound. "Ben, here, is always late for meetings, and his phone calls always run too long. Keeping him to a schedule is nearly impossible. He forgets to sign the paperwork I give him, and generally is a pain in my ass."

For about the millionth time, Bennett wondered why he kept Maudie around. Oh yes, because her fiancé had been in the military, and had been killed. She'd been desperate for work. He reminded himself that he admired her honesty.

"Stop gushing about me, Maudie. It'll go to my head. Now, please clear my calendar for the next hour. I want to bring Halle up to speed on things. No interruptions."

Maudie crossed her arms. "Fine." But he saw faint speculation on her face. It wasn't often he locked himself in the office with someone.

"See you later, Maudie," Hadley said.

He waved Hadley ahead of him and she sauntered into his office. His gaze dropped down to her legs and those sky-high heels she wore. His damn fantasies stirred.

Then he caught Maudie eyeing him.

Bennett cleared his throat and followed Hadley into the office. He closed the door behind them.

She stood by his desk, studying his office.

He tried to see it through her eyes. It wasn't sleek or glossy. The walls had old military antiques hanging or resting on shelves. There were old helmets, vests, canteens, and other items. The most modern thing was his big wooden desk.

And his brain delivered him the perfect image of Hadley in that dress, bent over his desk, his hands running up—

Hell.

He circled the polished wood and sat to hide his raging erection.

Hadley perused the shelves, then stopped by a framed photograph. It was a picture of Bennett and Hamed. It had been after a successful mission. They'd rescued a bunch of Afghan kids from a local warlord. They were still in their uniforms, hot and sweaty, arms slung over each other's shoulders and smiling.

He stayed still and silent. Fuck, he missed the guy.

She looked back at him.

"My Afghan interpreter." His throat tightened, dark memories stirring. Ones that always left him bleeding.

Hadley strode back his way, but like she sensed he didn't want to talk about it, she didn't ask any questions. He was grateful.

A part of him wanted to reach for her. Slide an arm around her and rest his face against her flat stomach. He wanted to touch her, whisper things to her that would make her writhe. He wanted to discover what she wanted, craved, and give it to her.

You shouldn't even be breathing her air, with stained hands like yours, let alone thinking about touching her. The voice in his head sounded snide.

As he always did, he gritted his teeth and ignored it. Work always helped.

A closed laptop and cell phone rested on the side of his desk.

"These are Archie Martin's?" she asked.

He nodded.

Hadley dropped into a seat on the other side of his desk and pulled the laptop toward her. "You've got the passwords?"

"They're unlocked. They both belong to the company and my IT team's been over them. There are no obvious signs of corporate espionage or terrorist leanings."

She tapped on the keyboard. "Most people are good at lying, Knightley. You should know that."

He sighed and sat back in his chair. "Are you always this cynical?"

She flicked him a glance. "Yes."

"Do you trust anyone, Hadley?"

"Trust is for fools." She tapped some more.

"I'd say Archie's pretty transparent. Slightly geeky, bit of a klutz, good at his job. If he was playing me, he's an Oscar-worthy actor."

"People tend to see what they want to see."

Something pinged on his radar. "Did someone fool you, Hadley?" Did someone break her trust and start the foundations of those walls of hers?

He saw a flash of emotion in her eyes before she hid it. "We aren't talking about me." She tapped her nails on the desk. "Maybe someone got to him. Manipulated or blackmailed him. He seemed very unhappy that you were at the party. I don't think he wanted to hurt you."

Bennett forced himself to focus on Archie, and nodded. It was a small comfort that his own employee hadn't wanted to kill him.

"I don't see anything here," she said. "But I know someone who can help us. I'll call the Sentinel Security goddess of hacking and tech."

"A hacker?"

"A good one."

"Go ahead." They needed answers.

Hadley rose, pressing her phone to her ear and paced. That tempting body moved past him, back and forth.

Pure torture.

"Hex. I have a job for you." Hadley ran down what they needed. Then she put her cell phone on the desk and put it on speaker.

"I need access to the Secura system," Hex said.

"Sure thing," Bennett said, pulling the laptop closer.

"Ooh, that British accent." He glanced down and saw the face of the woman on the screen of Hadley's phone. She had dark hair with pink tips that brushed her shoulders, and a cute face.

"I have a British accent," Hadley said.

"Sorry, I'm not into girls." Hex's nose wrinkled. "If I was though, I'd do you."

Hadley rolled her eyes. "Thanks. I think."

"Okay, Mr. Hottie Billionaire, I'm in."

"Ignore her," Hadley said.

"You don't think I'm a hottie billionaire?" he asked.

That earned him another eyeroll. "I'm not stroking your ego, Knightley."

"Uh-oh, you said the word stroking."

She snorted.

"I'm just a simple soldier, after all," he said. "It doesn't take much."

"You're not just a simple anything," she countered.

"You two are cute," Hex said, grinning.

"Have you got anything?" Hadley asked pointedly.

"I do. I'm still running several searches, but I found a few text messages. He messaged someone he saved as Kit. He talked about missing her, and seeing her in the newspaper with her husband and being jealous."

"Archie was seeing a married woman?" Bennett asked, shocked.

"There are only a few texts. Kit tells him not to use the phone. To email her."

"That sounds a bit fishy," Hadley said.

"Do former MI6 agents use the word fishy?" Bennett asked.

"I do. Anything in the emails, Hex?"

"The search is still running. And I'm cross-referencing newspaper articles from the date of the text message for anyone with Kit in their name."

Damn, this Hex was good. Bennett wondered if he could lure her away from Hawke.

Hadley tapped her nails on the desk again "I hope we're onto something here."

"If I could get in to talk with Archie, I'm sure I can get him to share," Bennett said.

"You know he's locked up tight," Hadley said. "He tried to blow up a lot of important people."

"It was a fake bomb."

"He didn't know that. From what David said, Archie's not well. I doubt you'd get anything coherent out of him."

Bennett raked a hand through his hair. "Someone did this to him. He's getting the best treatment, so there is always a chance he might be able to share something."

Hadley paused and he felt her gaze like a laser.

"The best treatment?" she asked.

He shrugged a shoulder. "He needs help."

"And you're paying for that?"

"He's one of mine," Bennett said.

She kept looking at him like he was some strange puzzle she couldn't put together. "He betrayed you."

"He was preyed on, because he worked for me."

"Okay, I found some emails to a kittycat99," Hex said. "Ahh...some are *very* interesting emails."

Hadley leaned over Bennett, her breast brushing his shoulder. He closed his eyes and counted to five.

"Interesting, how?" Hadley asked.

Hex waggled her eyebrows. "Like porn interesting."

Bennett focused on the screen and the emails that Hex had isolated. *Jesus.* Some of Archie and Kittycat's emails were rather X-rated.

Hadley gasped.

"Hell," Bennett muttered. "I didn't know Archie had it in him."

"A blow job in her car, sex in a park, sex in her bed when her husband was away on business, spanking." Hadley cleared her throat. "Sounds like Archie was...enthusiastic."

"Look at the earlier emails," Hex said. "She was working him hard."

Bennett saw how the woman was manipulating Archie, especially once sex was involved. Essentially grooming him. His stomach turned over.

"She was brainwashing him to her cause," Hadley said, reading through the emails. "To stop British military interference abroad."

"Got her!" Hex announced.

A picture popped up of a couple. The woman looked to be about fifty, with beautifully dyed, blonde hair, and looked well-groomed. She had high cheekbones and a charming smile.

"Shit. She has to be twice Archie's age," Bennett said.

Hex continued, "Lady Kitty Wentworth, wife of—"

"Ian Wentworth," Bennett said. "I've met him. He's friends with the prime minister. God."

"So why does Kitty Wentworth want to seduce Archie?" Hadley said.

"To get access to Secura," Hex said.

"She's working with an arms dealer?" Bennett asked skeptically.

Hadley crossed her arms. "Anyone can be radicalized. Even bored, rich housewives looking for some excitement in their lives." Hadley paused for a moment. "Or she could be a plant."

Hex made a sound. "I highly doubt some British society woman is a foreign agent."

"It's happened before."

The ice in Hadley's tone made him look at her. He saw a fine tension in her body.

"Hex, run her," Hadley said. "There must be a link to L'Orage."

"I've got something else," Hex said. "Kitty Wentworth is at a luncheon today at Scott's Restaurant, if you want to get a closer look at her."

Scott's was London's best seafood restaurant, located in Mayfair.

"I do," Bennett growled, looking at Hadley. "Hungry?"

She cocked a brow. "You can get a table at Scott's at the last minute?"

He smiled. "There are some benefits to being a hottie billionaire."

CHAPTER FOUR

H adley stood outside the Secura office, as she waited for Bennett's car to be brought around. She was on her phone, firing off a few messages to Hex for more info she needed.

He was standing beside her, hands on his hips and staring sightlessly at the traffic on the street. He'd put his suit jacket on, and of course, it made him look hotter. She wondered what would make him look less hot.

Doesn't matter how hot the man is, Hadley. You've seen plenty of hot guys, you've dated some, slept with a few. So what?

There were other qualities she valued more than how good a man looked.

A muscle ticked in his jaw. He was upset. *That*, she understood. Someone was targeting his company. She knew enough now to understand that it wasn't about the money. She suspected he was angrier that his shipments weren't getting to those who needed them.

Knightley wasn't like most very wealthy men she knew.

"Do you want to talk about it?" she asked.

"No."

"Do you want to swan into the best seafood restaurant in London, looking like a thundercloud?"

He blew out a breath and tossed her an annoyed look.

Damn, that made him look hotter, too. "I know you're pissed that L'Orage has infiltrated your company—"

Bennett sliced a hand through the air. "It's not just that. Archie's...impressionable, but a decent guy. They used him. This Wentworth woman screwed him over."

"We don't know the details yet."

Bennett made a sound.

"I have an undetectable bug with a built-in tracker," she said.

His face sharpened. "Really?"

"A little toy of Hex's. We need to get it on Kitty's phone."

"Oh, I'll get it on there." His voice was dark, full of promise.

She needed to distract him. If he didn't lighten up, he'd blow this. Kitty would take one look at him and see a predator on the hunt. "So, did your mother have a thing for Jane Austen?"

His head shot up. "What?"

"Bennett Knightley. Lizzie Bennet from my favorite Austen, *Pride and Prejudice*. Mr. Knightley from *Emma*."

"My father is responsible for the Knightley bit, but yes, my mother scarred me and my siblings for life."

Hadley smiled. "Tell me one of your brothers is named Fitzwilliam."

Bennett snorted and his lips quirked.

Ah. The distraction was working.

"No," he said.

"Wickham?"

He laughed. "No. But one of my brothers is Weston."

Hadley thought for a second. "From *Emma*."

He nodded. "And my other brother is Brandon."

"Colonel Brandon from *Sense and Sensibility*. Excellent."

"And I have a sister called Courtney."

"Hmm? From *Persuasion*?"

"Nope. General Courtney is from *Northanger Abbey*."

Hadley snapped her fingers. "So close."

A dark gray Maserati Quattroporte pulled up at the curb.

A big man got out of the driver's seat. He was wearing a suit, but Hadley could tell instantly that the man would prefer being in cargo pants.

"Ex-military," she murmured. "SAS."

The man had dark skin, shaved black hair, and a dark beard. He jerked his chin at her.

"Henry Bretton," Bennett said. "Halle Atwood. She's Secura's new head of communications."

"A pleasure," Hadley said.

As the man took a few steps toward her, she noted he had a prosthetic leg but hid it well. Clearly this was another person Bennett had given a job to after they'd left the military.

"Bullshit," Henry said.

Hadley blinked.

Bennett made a sound and opened the back door of the car. "Fuck, have some manners, Henry."

"No way she's a communications manager." Henry's voice was a deep rasp.

He circled back to the driver's seat.

Hadley slipped into the back seat and Bennett climbed in after her. Suddenly, the luxury car felt far smaller.

Henry pulled into traffic, heading for Mayfair.

Her phone pinged and she glanced down at the message from Hex. Her chest tightened. She'd guessed as much.

"Okay, Henry, this is Hadley Lockwood," Bennett said. "Former MI6, currently works for Sentinel Security out of New York."

Henry grunted.

"Knightley, I'm undercover," she said. "You're not supposed to tell everybody who I am."

"Henry here knows everything. Hadley's helping find whoever the fuck is betraying Secura."

Henry grunted again. "Good."

She sank back against the leather seat. "We think it links to an arms dealer called L'Orage." She wasn't sure she was happy trusting this Henry.

The man's curse was low and rough. He met Hadley's gaze in the rearview mirror. "I'm not going to share intel with a fucking arms dealer. What Knightley didn't share is that I'm his best friend. And he saved my life overseas. I'd die for him."

"He gets mushy like this a lot," Bennett said. "It's embarrassing."

Henry ignored him.

But Hadley saw clearly that Henry Bretton was not lying. He would do whatever he had to do to protect Knightley.

"We're going to surveil a society woman who might have links to L'Orage," Hadley said.

"This woman used Archie," Bennett clipped out. "She's older, married."

"Fuck. A cougar."

"She cooked him," Bennett said unhappily.

He was really upset about the young man, even though Archie had betrayed him and Secura.

Hadley shifted on the seat, glancing sideways at him. "You're paying for Archie's medical treatment, and you hired him one of the best legal firms in London." That little tidbit had been in Hex's last message.

Bennett sank back in his seat. "So?"

Helping someone who hurt him. She couldn't get a handle on him and it left her off kilter. He wasn't just some rough, former soldier. He wasn't just a rich, entitled businessman.

He turned his head and met her gaze.

It hit her like a punch to the gut.

She quickly looked straight ahead.

Bennett cleared his throat. "I got this for you." He held something out.

Hadley looked down at the small, compact umbrella. She took it, bemused. "What's this for?"

"I noticed yesterday at MI6 that your hair was damp.

You've obviously been in New York too long and forgot that it's always bloody raining here."

She took the umbrella and stared at him. *He'd noticed her hair was damp?*

"It's small enough to fit in your handbag."

After a long pause, she swallowed. "Thank you."

Their gazes locked again. They leaned toward each other.

A loud clearing of a throat made them both straighten.

"Fuck," Bennett muttered, glaring toward the front seat.

"So, Scott's?" Henry prompted, smoothly changing lanes to avoid a turning car.

"Kitty Wentworth is having a luncheon at Scott's," Hadley said. "Knightley and I are going to check her out."

Henry grunted. "I'll hang close by in case you need backup."

"He's so clingy," Bennett said.

She couldn't stop her laugh.

"I'm going to hit you later," Henry drawled. "You're still just an annoying git."

"Ha, remember who whipped your arse in the gym during our last sparring session?" Bennett said.

"Boys," Hadley said. "How about we focus?"

The humor leaked out of Bennett's handsome face. "Oh, believe me, I plan to find out exactly what Kitty Wentworth knows."

SCOTT'S RESTAURANT had an understated elegance about it. Hadley appreciated the classy front to the restaurant—with a dark awning and a unique, round window. She'd been there once or twice with her family.

Henry dropped her and Bennett off out in front. Bennett helped her out of the car, then tucked her arm into his.

She eyed him, trying to ignore the feel of him so close. Heat pumped off him, and unsurprisingly, there were hard muscles under his suit. The billions of dollars hadn't made him soft.

As they entered the restaurant, she saw the place was filled with people. The inside was as sleek as the outside. A staff member spotted him and rushed to greet them.

"Mr. Knightley, a pleasure to see you again," the man in a black uniform said. "We have your table ready."

"Thank you, Wilson," Bennett said.

They handed their coats over, then were led to a table by the window. She took in the long, marble bar and the other tables covered in snowy-white tablecloths.

The waiter held her seat out for her, and she smiled, but her gaze shifted to the long table of well-dressed ladies nearby. Kitty Wentworth sat at one end, chatting with another woman. Hadley heard Bennett order them drinks.

Kitty was smiling, unconcerned, even though she'd ruined a young man's life and was working with an arms dealer intent on causing chaos.

Hadley glanced back at Bennett, and saw he was watching Kitty, as well. His mouth firmed into a flat line, and a look entered his eyes. A hunter sensing his prey.

"Hey." Hadley reached across the table and took his hand.

He gripped hers, and she felt the calluses on his palm. No, definitely not soft.

"She's just sitting there, without a fucking care in the world," he said sharply.

"We don't know exactly how involved she is yet." Hadley studied him carefully. "It's not your fault Archie made a bad decision and got sucked into this."

Bennett blew out a breath. "I hired him. He got discharged from the Navy, and was lost. He was targeted because of me."

"No, he was targeted because L'Orage needed a way into Secura, and Archie was a weak link."

Now, Bennett sucked in a breath. He looked at their hands and turned her palm over, stroking it.

Hadley fought back a shiver. "I know most of your staff members are former military or family of military."

He shifted in his seat. "So?"

"You're a mother hen, collecting up little chicks."

He stared at her with a faint scowl.

"I'm starting to think you are a good guy, Knightley."

He leaned in, tightening his hold on her hand. "Not always."

She just watched him.

"I'm not a saint, Hadley. I needed employees, they needed jobs. They ensure my company is a success, and I make a lot of money."

"We both know that's not why you do it."

"I do it to help, but...I do it for me too. It helps keep

me level." His eyes darkened. "I saw shit, did shit, and the memories never go away."

Secura was his way of keeping the nightmares at bay. She understood. Work did the same for her.

"I can't let anyone threaten my work or my people." His gaze strayed back to Kitty.

"She might get nervous if she sees you here," Hadley said.

He looked back at her. "Coincidence. This is the best seafood restaurant in London, and clearly a place I frequent. Lunching with my new head of communications makes sense."

"You're going to get a reputation for office hanky-panky, if you keep this up." She tried to tug her hand free.

He smiled and held tight. "One look at you, and no one would blame me." He traced the sensitive spot between her fingers.

She should be immune. She hadn't let a man affect her like this in...forever. Not since Casper had shattered her trust. "Oh, so you indulge in office affairs often?"

He pulled her hand closer and leaned in. She got a whiff of his cologne, and it made her think of a dark, dense forest.

"Never. But it makes a good cover for us spending a lot of time together."

She was saved from the discussion when a server brought their drinks. She discreetly kept her gaze on Kitty.

"She doesn't seem troubled or nervous," Hadley said.

Bennett grunted unhappily.

Hadley ordered grilled Dover sole and Bennett

ordered seared Sea Bass. The meal arrived swiftly, and they ate as the table of women ordered more champagne.

"We need to get a closer look at her," he said. "Or we can't get that bug in place."

Hadley saw Kitty rise and head toward the bar. "Now might be the chance." She went to rise.

"No, I'll go," he said.

She studied his face. He was too rugged to be considered classically handsome, but it only made him look better to her. "Are you going to keep your cool?"

He rose, leaned down, and pressed his mouth to her ear. Her stupid heart jolted.

"I was SAS, remember? I'm good at compartmentalizing and doing whatever I need to do to get the mission done."

She turned her head. Their lips were an inch apart. "The SAS is also good at blowing shit to hell."

His lips curled. "I promise, no explosions."

He stalked across the restaurant. Hadley was not surprised to see many female gazes follow him. God, that ass was something. She realized she'd picked up *ass* versus *arse* from Hex. The hacker was a bad influence.

Hadley sipped her water. When she glanced over, Bennett was leaning against the bar, smiling.

And Kitty Wentworth was lapping up the attention.

Hadley's hand tightened on her glass. She watched Bennett's smile widen. He poured his charm on the woman.

He was probably practiced at it. Kitty leaned in, practically rubbing her breasts against him. Bennett said something, then reached out and touched Kitty's bare arm.

God, he didn't have to go over the top.

Maybe he liked it? Maybe he liked having every woman fawning over him.

Focus on the job, Hadley.

Suddenly, Kitty paused. She stroked Bennett's arm and pulled out her cell phone.

Ah. Just what they needed.

They needed to get the bug on that phone.

With a wave, Kitty headed toward the ladies' room.

Hadley rose. She moved toward Bennett.

"Have fun?" There was a bite of acid in her voice, more than she'd intended.

He arched a brow. "I just let her do her thing."

"It looked like you enjoyed it."

His gaze narrowed. "I did what I had to." He leaned in. "Who trashed your trust in mankind? You're so quick to believe the worst of everyone."

His words stung. "I believe in reality."

"Reality is that you're jealous."

"Hardly." She sucked in a breath. Was that what she was feeling? *Oh, God.*

Bennett leaned in, frustration on his face. "You're lying to yourself. You hide behind those walls of yours, keeping everyone at a distance, fighting what you're feeling. Do you ever bloody let go, Hadley? Ever just feel without running it through a hundred filters?"

The arrow hit its target, slashed at her, and she hissed in a breath.

Bennett shook his head. "Fuck. I didn't mean—"

"I need to get the bug on that phone." She swept past him.

In the ladies' room, she saw that one stall was occupied. She heard a hushed voice talking.

Hadley pulled out her lipstick and leaned into the mirror. She tried to push Bennett's words away. The toilet flushed, and Kitty emerged.

She was attractive. The high cheekbones and blonde hair caught the eye, but she also exuded an energy that caught the gaze. Hadley could see how a young, confused man could be swept in.

Hadley met Kitty's gaze in the mirror and nodded. The other woman set her phone down on the counter beside the sink and washed her hands.

Hadley pulled Hex's bug off the lipstick tube. Then she fumbled the lipstick and it clattered down beside the phone.

"Oh no. I'm so clumsy." She touched Kitty's phone, and quickly pressed the thin, plastic bug onto the back of it. Then Hadley grabbed her lipstick tube. "I don't want to lose this. This shade is my favorite, and Gucci doesn't make it anymore."

"Oh, I *hate* when they discontinue your favorites." With a nod, Kitty left.

Hadley smiled into the mirror. *Got you.*

She exited the restroom and found Bennett waiting in the narrow hall.

"What are you doing back here?" she asked.

"I wanted to check that you were okay."

She made an angry sound. "Do you really think a woman like Kitty Wentworth could take me?"

"It's not that. I was a dick before, at the bar."

"All men are dicks."

"You aren't that cynical."

"I am."

Suddenly, Kitty's voice sounded close by. She was talking on the phone again, and getting closer.

"Yes, Knightley's here. No. He has no clue. I think he was here for a work lunch. It's a popular place."

Oh, shit. "If she sees us—"

"Here." Bennett yanked open a door. It was a storage cupboard. Tablecloths and napkins were neatly stacked on tall shelves. Cleaning supplies sat heaped in a corner.

They slipped inside and the door closed behind them, enveloping them in darkness.

Outside, they heard Kitty walk past, her voice muffled.

"You think she's talking to L'Orage?" Bennett asked.

"We'll find out soon with the bug in place."

Kitty's voice faded away.

"Sounds like it's clear." Hadley tried the door. It didn't budge. "Oh, hell."

Bennett pushed up behind her. "What?"

"The door's locked, and there's no handle on this side."

"You're joking," he said.

"No."

They were trapped.

CHAPTER FIVE

"Let me see." Bennett moved through the darkness and leaned over Hadley. He pressed a hand against the door and just felt a smooth plate. No lock to pick. "Shit."

"Can you call Henry?"

He saw the vague outline of her face in the darkness. "Yes." He reached for his pocket and cursed.

She made a sound. "What now?"

"My phone is in my jacket pocket, and my jacket is—"

"Hanging in the coat closet," she finished.

He'd taken it off when they arrived, and bloody forgot about his phone.

He heard her rummage in her bag. "I have mine. Do you know Henry's number?"

"Without my phone, I don't know anybody's number."

"I'll message Hex." The screen lit up.

"Did you get the bug in place?" he asked.

She looked up at him, her face awash with blue light. "Of course."

God, he liked that self-assured tone. His cock *really* liked it.

He liked everything about this woman.

She shifted and sat on a box. Bennett followed and sat beside her. Their legs brushed, and her citrus and floral perfume teased him. He closed his eyes and counted to ten.

"I'm sure you have reasons not to trust easily," he said quietly. "I had no right to poke at you about it."

She was quiet for a moment. "Most of what you said was right. I don't trust easily, and I have my reasons."

"Who was he?"

She sighed. "A foreign agent. I didn't know that when I was falling in love with him."

The thought of Hadley loving any man made Bennett's gut tight as a rock. He hated it. But the thought of some shithead using her was worse.

"You're lying, too," she said. "The charming 'lord of the manor' thing you have going on—others might fall for it, but not me."

He stiffened. "I am who I am, Hadley."

"Secura, everything you do, is calculated to get your way."

"I won't apologize for that. My way means soldiers and their support staff in shitty places have a better chance at survival. They don't end up bleeding in the fucking dirt."

Silence reigned in the enclosed space.

Bennett heaved in a breath. *Damn*. He hadn't meant to lose it.

"Who did you lose?" she asked quietly.

Hell, who hadn't he lost. "Battle brothers, some Afghan soldiers I worked with...and my Afghan interpreter. Smart guy with a sharp sense of humor. Hamed wanted to help his country find a better future. He wanted to give his little girl a chance at a life with some freedom. The tough bastard saved my life more than once, and helped our team countless times. I used to give him some of our gear. The shit he was supplied with was a joke." He paused, gut tightening.

"Bennett," she said softly.

"We were at a village to meet an informant. One of my men, our new guy, Paul Davies, triggered an IED, then we came under fire. I was injured in the explosion, crawling to get to cover. My team was all returning fire. Paul was blown to bits. He was so damn young. And Hamed—" Bennett hadn't been able to save his friend or the young man under his command. Guilt chewed at him. It often did when he stopped, slowed down, or wasn't working.

A slim hand covered his. He grabbed her like a lifeline.

He swallowed. "Hamed was torn to shreds. He'd given the vest I gave him to a younger, new interpreter. He was wearing a shitty one."

"I'm sorry."

"The explosion ripped through his vest like paper. And we never found Paul's body, just...his hand. He was a good kid, excited to have made the SAS, was *always* talking. He loved quoting lines from old movies. Used to drive us crazy."

"It wasn't your fault, Bennett. You know that."

They hadn't been the first people he'd lost, but their deaths had been the last he could cope with. "I know that in my head, but it's harder for the rest of me to accept." He drew in a breath. "I'll never, ever stop regretting that I couldn't save them. I'd promised Hamed's wife I'd keep him safe, and I wasn't even fucking on my feet when he was dying."

"You started Secura because of your friend."

"Yes, he was a big reason. Hamed and I always talked about how so much more was needed than just guns and grenades. We'd seen too many people making do with crap gear. Too many who were sick and uncomfortable under already shitty circumstances."

"What happened to your interpreter's wife and little girl, Bennett?"

He shifted on the box. "They live here, in the UK."

"You brought them over here."

He didn't reply. It'd been the least he could do for Hamed.

"Hmm. So, you really are a good guy, Bennett Knightley."

He grunted. "I told you not to go making me a saint."

"Saint Bennett," she teased.

He leaned closer to her. "If you knew what I think every time I see you, you wouldn't use the word good."

Her fingers tightened on his. He thought she wouldn't say anything, but her voice cut through the darkness.

"What do you think when you see me?"

His heart beat hard. He swiveled, caging her legs with his. "I think you're so damn beautiful that I can't think straight. That I want to touch you. Everywhere. I'm half hard anytime you're in the room."

"Bennett—"

Damn, he heard the desire in her voice. "When you walked into my office today, all I wanted to do was bend you over my desk and push your dress up. Control has been the cornerstone of my life since I joined the military, and you shred it."

He heard her fast breathing. "Knightley—"

He groaned. "Even when you say my name, with that slight edge, that hints you either want to hit me or kiss me, it gets to me."

"We have a mission. An important one."

"I know. My cock just hasn't gotten the memo yet."

"*Bennett.*"

"I know L'Orage is dangerous, Hadley. No one wants to uncover whoever the hell is betraying me and Secura more than I do. But it doesn't stop me wanting you. It doesn't stop me liking your sharp mind, your insane competence at your job, your sexy poise, your gorgeous body."

Silence. He waited for her to punch him.

"Damn you, Knightley." She gripped the front of his shirt, then she moved. In the blink of an eye, she straddled him and sank down on his lap.

Oh, fuck. He clamped his hands on her arse. Her mouth nipped his jaw and they both made hungry, urgent sounds. Arousal was a hard, dark beat through his blood.

He turned his head and took her mouth with his.

The taste of her hit him hard. Her hands sank into his hair, her hips rolling against him. She ground down on his raging erection.

She made a husky sound and bit his lip.

Yes. Fuck, yes.

Suddenly, the door opened and light flooded in.

"If this is the best way to find a rogue arms dealer, I've been doing my job wrong," a deep voice said.

HADLEY FROZE, her body glued against Bennett's hard one, and the very large cock pressed between her legs. She licked her lips and tasted him on her tongue.

She dragged in a few breaths. *Nope.* She took another deep one. Then she turned and looked at Killian in the doorway.

"Please be a figment of my imagination," she said.

"Sorry," Killian replied. "Hex called me and said you two needed an assist."

Her boss wore his usual cool, impassive look that he used to scare the shit out of everyone. But she knew him well enough to know he was amused.

She climbed off Bennett and straightened her skirt.

Bennett stayed sitting, and she guessed he needed a little more time to be...presentable.

"We were just..." Bennett trailed off.

Hadley looked at him. "Go on. I want to hear what you've got."

He coughed. "I've got nothing."

"How about humping on a box?" Killian suggested.

Hadley straightened and tossed her head back. She'd been in sticky situations before. "We were avoiding Kitty and managed to get locked in here."

Killian made a sound. "An experienced former MI6 agent and a former SAS operator can't get out of a locked room?"

"There's no lock or handle on this side!" Hadley said.

"I figured I shouldn't bust down a door in one of London's best restaurants," Bennett added.

"So kissing her was a better idea?" Killian asked.

"No, I kissed him," she confessed. "Now both of you be quiet." She strode past Killian and ran into Henry.

Bennett's best friend was grinning at her, his teeth white against his dark skin.

"Don't you say a thing," she snapped.

"I was just going to say that Ben has your lipstick smeared on his face," Henry said.

Hadley made a sound, swiveled, and strode back into the ladies' room. The reflection in the mirror showed a woman who'd just been thoroughly ravished.

What the hell were you thinking, Hadley Jane? Making out with a billionaire in a dark cupboard.

She hadn't been thinking, that was the problem.

She fixed her face, and re-did her lipstick. The men were waiting outside the restaurant. The Maserati was parked nearby.

"All right?" Killian asked.

"I'm fine. Kitty?"

"Left a couple minutes ago." Killian said. "The bug's in place?"

Hadley nodded, then glanced at Bennett. She couldn't read the look on his face. He'd wiped the lipstick off, but his hair was still disheveled, like fingers had been clenched in it.

Yeah, her fingers.

Henry stood behind Bennett, looking amused. *Asshole*.

She sucked in a breath. "We'd better get back to the office and see if Hex can get anything useful off the bug."

Bennett nodded. "Thanks, Killian."

Her boss jerked his chin, and slid one hand into his pocket. He looked at Hadley. "Stay out of trouble."

His tone left no doubt that he included Bennett as trouble.

"That's usually what you have to tell Hades, not me." Matteo "Hades" Mancini charged into any dangerous situation with a grin. "I can handle trouble."

"I know you can, but you have a habit of trying to do it all alone." Killian touched her shoulder. "You're not alone, Hadley."

With another sharp nod, her boss strode off.

Henry moved to the driver's side of the Maserati. Bennett held the back door of the car open for her.

She slid in and he followed.

"Hadley—"

She held up a hand. "Please don't."

She saw his mouth tighten. Thankfully, the drive was

mercifully short, and he didn't try to engage her in conversation.

In the Secura building, they strode into his office.

She moved straight to the laptop on the desk and flicked it open. "I need to check that Hex has the bug active."

"Hadley, are you going to ignore what happened?" he asked.

She didn't look up. "Yes. It was a kiss, that's it. Ill-advised, and badly timed."

She heard a frustrated sound. Now, she looked up. He was running his hands through his hair.

"You can turn it off that easily?" he growled.

"No, but I'm good at compartmentalizing, too." She tapped the keyboard. Her pulse was racing, but she didn't want him to know that.

"Apparently, I'm not. I can still taste you. Feel the sweet curves of your arse." He stepped closer.

Heat flashed through her, and she took a hasty step back and hit his executive chair. It rolled away.

A slow smile curled across his face. "Ah, not as good at compartmentalizing as you'd like me to believe, Ms. Lockwood?"

She straightened, trying to ignore the memory of his deep voice telling her that he fantasized about bending her over his desk. The desk right beside her.

"This isn't happening, Knightley. We have a mission. We have to find L'Orage before he destroys your company and so many lives."

Bennett looked away and muttered a curse.

"Hello?" Hex's voice came from the laptop. "Please

tell me you banged the billionaire." The hacker grinned on the screen.

Hadley closed her eyes and fought the urge to pinch the bridge of her nose.

"Oops." Hex sounded unrepentant. "He's right there, isn't he?"

Bennett circled the desk. "Hello, Hex."

"Hi. Sorry."

"There's been no banging yet," Bennett said. "I'm working on it."

Hadley glared at him.

Hex clapped her hands together. "Oh, man. I need to get out of the office more and find a billionaire for myself."

"The bug?" Hadley asked between clenched teeth. "And there'll be no banging, because I'm going to strangle Knightley. No one will ever find the body."

Hex looked like she was trying not to laugh.

Bennett winked. "I get giddy when she flirts like this."

Now Hex burst out laughing.

"If you two are done?" Hadley said.

"Right. The bug and built-in tracker are live. We'll see where she goes. It does transmit some audio, but you need to be close to pick it up."

Hadley pressed a hand to the desk. "Acknowledged. Where is she now?"

"Her home in Chelsea. I'll keep an eye on her, and look for any unusual movements. If anything comes up, I'll contact you."

There was a knock on the office door. Maudie pushed

it open and scowled at them. "You two are due in conference room one for a meeting."

Hadley flashed a smile. "We're on our way, Maudie. Thank you."

Bennett's assistant sniffed and closed the door.

"Thanks, Hex," Hadley said.

The hacker gave them a jaunty salute, and ended the call.

"Let's get to the meeting." She met Bennett's gaze. "From here on out, we're professionals. No touching, no kissing. We have a bad guy to catch."

"If you insist, Ms. Lockwood."

His quick grin and agreement annoyed her, but she also didn't trust it one little bit.

She knew the motto of the SAS was "Who dares wins," and she knew that Bennett Knightley never gave up.

CHAPTER SIX

H e let himself into his penthouse.

Bennett tossed his keys on the hall table, and the lights clicked on automatically.

He was tired, and frustration was a hard ball in his gut.

Thoughts of Hadley weren't far away. He stripped off his jacket and tossed it over the couch. He crossed the wooden floor to the built-in bar, grabbed a Waterford crystal glass, and a bottle of his Balvenie 40-year-old Scotch. He splashed a healthy amount into the glass, swirled, and took a large sip.

He'd spent the afternoon watching Hadley in meetings, trying to keep his gaze off her. He'd held her in his arms now, had his hands on her, so he knew exactly how she felt. He didn't think he'd quite succeeded not looking taken with her. Hadley had sent him some hot glares—which hadn't helped. And his CFO had been shooting him a few funny looks.

He sipped some more Scotch, and moved to the

living room windows. His curved balcony outside was a favorite place to spend time in the summer, but right now it was still too cold.

Hyde Park was a dark space ahead, with the glittering lights of the city in the distance.

His temples throbbed with a headache. All the emotion and stress had to go somewhere.

He sank into an armchair. "Lights off."

The lights dimmed away, leaving him in the dark.

He'd started Secura with one goal. To help. Help the people who sacrificed to serve their countries and protect other people.

It had filled the dark, gaping hole inside him. The one where his nightmares lurked. He closed his eyes. He saw Hamed's face, Paul's, and now Archie's.

Why the fuck had this L'Orage resurfaced and targeted him? Why was he messing with Secura?

Bennett knew he had to turn it off. He needed to recharge and start the fight again tomorrow. He'd learned that valuable lesson in the SAS. You had to grab rest and sleep where you could, to recharge the batteries.

As he swirled the last of his drink, he stared out the window sightlessly, his thoughts turning to Hadley.

Damn. He drained the rest of the Scotch.

You don't deserve her. She deserves much better than you.

Yeah, yeah, I know. He pulled out his phone, and turned it over and over in his hand.

He wondered what she was doing. Unsurprisingly, she pulled off the new communications role perfectly. No one at Secura suspected she wasn't exactly what she said she was. Smart and competent were a sexy combination.

But did Hadley ever let her hair down? Did she ever let go of that control?

Some shithead had hurt her. Would she ever let a man hold her close, let him take care of her softer parts? They were there, he was sure of it, just heavily guarded. He wanted all her secrets, wanted to know every single thing about her.

Would you share all your ugly secrets with her?

His throat tightened. Then he grabbed the phone and stabbed at the screen.

"It's late, Mr. Knightley," her voice came through the line.

He closed his eyes. "I know. How did the afternoon go?"

"You hire good people. And I had an update from Hex. Kitty Wentworth went nowhere that sparked any alarm bells. She spent time at home, the gym, had friends over for a dinner party. Her son is getting married next weekend, in some big, swanky wedding at a country estate, so she's busy planning that."

Bennett grunted. "I'm sure it'll be a spectacle."

"Been to a few?"

"Yes. There are always lots of flowers and people in expensive clothes."

She snorted. "Like you can talk. I've seen your Savile Row suits."

"Pot meet kettle. You like good designers too, Ms. Lockwood."

"I like to shop, and I love getting a good deal." She paused. "You didn't call to discuss clothes."

He sighed. "I want us to find a lead. I want L'Orage to pay for Archie."

"I know."

"I want Kitty to pay as well. They broke him. He's a good kid."

"She will." There was sympathy in Hadley's voice. "And I do understand."

"You do?"

"Yes. L'Orage was responsible for the death of a fellow MI6 agent. We'd almost caught him, got too close, and his men shot Olivia." Hadley's breath hitched. "She was only a year younger than me, and a good friend."

He heard the pain in her voice. Wished he could comfort her. "I'm sorry, Hadley." His fingers tightened on the phone. "I wish you were here."

Silence. "We both know that's a monumentally bad idea."

"I don't think so. I think it's a very good idea." His voice turned gritty. "We'd be good, Hadley. You know it."

"I have self-control, Bennett. Sex tends to complicate things, and be a distraction. It makes you blind. Just look at Archie."

But Bennett detected something else in her voice. Something she wanted to keep hidden. "Is that what happened with the dickhead agent?"

More silence. For a second, he thought she'd hung up.

"He betrayed me." A whip of anger in her voice. "I was young, and I'm not anymore."

"Who was he?" Bennett's hand curled into a fist. This bastard had used her, betrayed her trust.

No, broken it. And now, Hadley Lockwood didn't trust any man.

"He was sent here to infiltrate MI6 and spy. He was handsome, caring, paid attention. I thought I was the luckiest girl in London."

Bennett already hated the guy.

"I was twenty-one, and had just started working at MI6. He'd been embedded in the UK for years. Educated here. He had a posh British accent, and a charming demeanor. I fell hard."

Bennett tasted oil in his mouth. "You loved him."

"I thought I did, but in that young, shiny way when you're twenty-something. It's not very deep, and it's not very real. He wasn't real. I caught him trying to break into my work laptop."

"What happened?"

"I told him I was calling the authorities. He attacked me."

Her voice was devoid of emotion and Bennett cursed.

"I'm alive and he isn't. I learned a very valuable lesson."

And that was the day she built her formidable armor.

Armor Bennett was determined to get through. He'd earn her trust, dammit.

"Sex with me is going to complicate things...in a good way," he said. "And it's definitely going to be pleasurable. We can fuck each other's brains out and still get the mission done, Hadley."

"*Bennett—*"

"I want to touch every inch of you, Hadley. Learn what you like, make you moan with pleasure."

He heard her swift intake of air.

"I want to give you pleasure beyond your wildest dreams. I want you, Hadley. Not the agent, not the whip-smart specialist, just you. The woman."

There was no sound, but he knew she was listening.

"No walls between us. Just you and me. Give yourself over to me, let me have you. You can embrace everything you want."

"God." Her voice was a little shaky. "You're even better than I guessed."

He frowned. "At what?"

"Doing everything to get what you want. I knew you were dangerous. Ruthless."

"I'm not a danger to you."

Her laugh had a sharp edge. "Yes, you are."

"I won't betray your trust." His patience slipped. "I can give you what I don't think you've ever allowed yourself. You can trust me, Hadley. You can let go and I'll catch you."

"So dangerous," she whispered.

He smiled, feeling a little lighter.

"Why?" she asked. "Why do you want me?"

His throat was thick. "Because when I'm with you, life seems brighter. The nightmares seem farther away. Everything seems worth it."

He heard her quick breath.

Then his phone pinged.

"Message?" she asked.

He swiped at the screen and looked at the phone. Then he cursed.

"Bennett?" Her voice turned serious.

"Another shipment just went missing."

"No," she said.

His anger roared back. "I need to go."

"If you need help, call me."

He blew out a breath. "Thanks."

"Good night, Mr. Knightley."

"Dream of me, Ms. Lockwood."

THE NEXT MORNING, Hadley strode into the Secura office in her favorite black skirt suit, with a cream blouse and black pumps. She cradled her phone, and a takeout coffee from %Arabica, her favorite London coffee shop.

"Morning, Halle," Penny, the communications assistant called out.

Hadley lifted her coffee in salute. She scanned the office for Bennett, but there was no sign of him.

"Halle." A young man from the communications team made his way to her. "Meeting in ten minutes in conference room one."

"Thanks, Jack. Have you seen Bennett?"

Jack's nose wrinkled. "He's busy on the phone. Something's going down and it isn't good. He's like a bear with a wounded...well, everything."

She nodded. *Shit.* Clearly he hadn't recovered the last shipment.

She dumped her things in her office and grabbed her

tablet. She headed for Bennett's office and spotted Henry.

"Any news?" she asked quietly.

Henry looked pissed. "No. He's been on the phone all night. They almost caught the shipment on the highway, but the bastards got away. He's talking with MI6 right now. We need to catch these fuckers."

Hadley nodded. Archie was locked up, which meant someone else at Secura was working for L'Orage.

"Halle!" someone called. "Meeting."

"Coming," she called back.

She glanced into Bennett's office. He was standing in his suit trousers and a blue shirt, one hand on a lean hip and the phone pressed to his ear.

He was in profile, his body stiff. He was barking into the phone, stressed and pissed.

He looked good though. She mentally rolled her eyes, but in her head she was remembering his sexy voice on the phone last night. All the things he'd said. She felt a pulse low in her belly.

Great. Going into a meeting with damp panties was not what she needed.

Shaking her head, she hurried to conference room one.

The morning turned into a rush of meetings. When she finally got back to her desk, she found a salad that her assistant had left for her.

She also found a small box of chocolates. Since they were from Pierre Marcolini, her favorite chocolatier, she didn't think they were from Penny. Hadley opened the box and found neat colored rows of Les Coeurs. Small, heart-shaped chocolates. She grabbed her favorite and popped it in her mouth.

The flavor of dark chocolate ganache and raspberry exploded in her mouth.

Damn you, Knightley. He was trying to seduce her with little gifts.

She ate her salad, and several more chocolates, while she shot off messages to Hex.

Her email pinged. It was a message from Gabbi. It contained a photo of Gabbi and a smiling little Cora from Nightingale House. The African-American girl was holding up a little sign that said "I miss you, Hadley."

Hadley felt a pang under her heart and smiled. She missed her visits to the shelter as well. She saved the picture on her phone.

A message from Hex popped up. Kitty Wentworth wasn't doing anything remotely interesting. Right now, she was at a day spa.

Hadley let herself imagine having the time to get a massage and a facial.

Unfortunately, stopping criminals didn't leave her a lot of time for day spas.

She approached Bennett's office and Maudie stalked out.

The assistant scowled. "Wear armor if you're going in there."

Hmm. Hadley slipped inside.

"No." Bennett was on the phone again, his tone sharp as a blade. "I want the information *today*, not tomorrow." A pause. "That's not up for negotiation. Get it done." He slammed the desk phone down and dragged a hand through his hair.

"Rough day?" she asked.

His head snapped up. "I want to strangle someone, preferably L'Orage."

"The shipment?"

He sighed and dropped back into his chair. "Gone." His tone pulsated with contained rage. "We almost caught them, but the fuckers caused an accident on the M25, which blocked my security team."

"Anyone hurt?"

"Nothing major, thank God. So damn close." He sighed. "It was a big shipment, Hadley. I needed to get it to aid workers in Syria. *Fuck*."

Tension throbbed off him. He looked like he was going to snap.

She walked over to him. "We aren't going to let him win."

"He's already winning. I just had MI6 yelling at me. And a reporter is sniffing around."

She couldn't stop herself from stroking her hand across his shoulders. They were broad, but even being strong, the crap built-up to heavy levels.

"You're not alone, Bennett. I'm here, and Killian will bring in backup, if we need it." She rubbed her fingers at the base of his neck. "As soon as we snag a lead, we'll be on the trail."

He leaned his head forward, his muscles relaxing a little. "That feels good."

"Switch it off for five minutes."

"I can't. My company, my responsibility—"

"It won't fall apart without you for five minutes." She kneaded his shoulders and he gave a low groan.

Some of the tension bled out of him.

"How did you know my favorite chocolates?" she asked.

"That's—"

"Classified," she finished.

He shot her a tired smile. "Yes."

"Well, thank you."

He reached up and gripped one of her hands. "Come home with me tonight."

Hadley stilled. God, she was tempted to not be alone. Good sex would provide a hell of a lot of stress relief for both of them.

But put so much more at risk.

"It's still not a good idea," she said.

His shoulders slumped. "I knew you'd say that."

"Ben—"

His phone rang. He sucked in a breath. "I need to take that."

"And I have a meeting. This fake job is a lot of work."

He flashed her a tight smile. She couldn't help but touch his shoulder again, then headed out.

She heard his deep voice as he answered the phone.

Hadley ended up dealing with more meetings and calls. She traded messages with Hex, pulling Kitty Wentworth's life apart.

How the hell did a wealthy London society woman get involved with an arms dealer?

They'd find the connection.

Suddenly, she realized the office was emptying out.

"Hey, Halle." Jack peered into her office, smiling. "A few of us are heading to a bar around the corner for an after-work drink. Keen?"

Not really. She wanted to check in with Bennett.

She glanced out her door and saw that his office door was closed.

It was important she connect with the Secura employees. Subtly probe to see if they had any information on who might be leaking information on the company.

"A drink sounds good. Thanks, Jack."

He smiled, a flush on his cheeks. "Great."

Soon, Hadley found herself in a snug little bar around the corner from the office. The group of Secura employees were mostly from the communications team.

Jack took a sip of his beer. "Long day."

"The boss man still in the office?" someone asked.

"He's there late nearly every night," another woman said. "Classic workaholic."

"He's stressed about this shipment that went missing," another man said.

"Pissed, you mean," a woman noted.

Jack leaned forward. "I heard a whisper that maybe someone on the inside *leaked* the shipment details."

"*No,*" Penny, the assistant from the comms team, murmured.

Hadley paused, ensuring she wore a shocked expression. "Who? Everyone seems to love their jobs, and despite his workaholic tendencies, Bennett is a good boss."

"With a fine arse," Penny said.

Everyone looked at her. She froze mid sip of her cocktail. "Man, this is strong." She shook the glass. "Did I say that thought out loud?"

"You're not wrong, though," another woman agreed.

"So who is leaking the shipment details? This Archie guy?" Hadley asked.

"Poor Archie," Jack said. "I don't know what the hell went wrong with him. If I'd had to pick anyone to leak company secrets, it wouldn't have been Archie."

"Maybe someone hacked the computer system?" Penny said.

"I don't know," an older guy grunted. "Bennett's being shifty lately, secretive. Maybe he did it himself."

There were scoffing sounds around the table.

"It's his company," Jack exclaimed.

"He's SAS," the old guy said. "Nothing gets past the SAS. Have you seen him? He's alert. Always knows what the hell's going on."

Hadley felt a cold shiver.

"He could be fooling the lot of us," the man continued. "All those late nights at the office, alone. Where there's smoke there's fire, I always say."

Jack scoffed. "That makes no sense. Why?"

The older man shrugged. "Insurance? For kicks? Who knows?"

For a second, Hadley was thrust back ten years. To when she'd been young, fresh, and idealistic. So proud to be working at MI6. And so entranced by a charming young London banker.

She'd ignored the little niggles or explained Casper's quirks away. The phone calls that he hadn't answered in front of her, or the ones he took where she wouldn't over-hear. Or the times he'd gotten in late, or she'd found him up in the middle of the night, saying he couldn't sleep.

Finally, she'd caught him at her laptop and every-thing had become clear. She'd seen the signs, she just hadn't wanted to believe.

She'd ignored the obvious.

Her stomach turned over. Was she doing that now too? Was Bennett a good actor as well?

"Owen, you and your conspiracies," Penny said with a huff. "Bennett would rather chew off his hand than hurt Secura."

Hadley cleared her throat, forcing down the sick feel-ing. "Well, everyone, I need to head out. See you tomorrow."

CHAPTER SEVEN

Bennett muttered a curse and sank back in his chair. The office was dark and quiet. He liked being there late at night, once the place had emptied out.

He got more work done without people interrupting him constantly, and all the meetings. And often, he had international calls to make at odd hours. He needed to think about starting some overseas offices.

On top of that, there were some nights he wasn't good company, and didn't want to go home alone. Those were the nights when old memories—of gunfire, heat, and blood—wanted out.

He sighed. He'd been lucky not to end up with PTSD. He'd found ways to cope, and pouring himself into Secura had been the biggest help.

Now some bastard was threatening it.

He growled and stared blindly at the laptop screen. A friend in the Middle East had emailed him to report that they'd seen Secura vests on insurgents.

The fuckers. His gear was meant to protect the good guys, not the bad guys.

He wanted to punch something. His hands flexed. Then he saw movement in the doorway.

Hadley stood there. Of course, despite the long day, she still looked fabulous. That fitted skirt and blouse looked barely wrinkled. Her hair was up in an elegant twist.

"Working late?" she asked.

"I often do."

"So I hear."

He cocked a brow at her tone.

She shrugged a shoulder. "I had after-work drinks with the gang."

"Ah."

"They said you never go for drinks."

"I'm the boss. They don't really want me there. I can't be their friend, and they can't let their hair down around me."

"There's lots of speculation about the lost shipment. Everyone knows."

He grunted. "There's always office gossip. With what happened with Archie, and now this, I bet there's lots of talk."

She walked closer to his desk. "Some say you always work late. That you have your fingers in everything, and there's no way anyone could get anything past you."

Bennett cocked his head, his pulse starting to pound. "What are you getting at?"

"Some people are speculating that you could be behind the lost shipments."

Anger and frustration geysered up inside him. He clenched his jaw, fighting for control.

"You'd like that, wouldn't you? It would prove that you're right to never trust anyone. That we're all arse-holes out to screw everyone over."

Despite his angry words, her face stayed calm and serene, her sharp gaze on his features.

Bennett thrust to his feet. He refused to admit he felt some hurt in the anger. "That dickhead did a number on you, didn't he, Hadley? You know what, keep your armor on. Stay distrusting and alone. Now get out."

She didn't move, instead she came closer.

"I'm not in the mood, Hadley."

She ran her fingers along his desk. "I didn't say I believed it."

He stilled.

"I don't trust easily, and yes, once upon a time I learned a soul-shattering lesson. Once, I let a man into my home, into my body, into my heart, but to him, I was just a means to an end. Despite that, I consider myself a good judge of character. I've seen manipulative assholes, I've seen evil assholes, and greedy, power-hungry assholes. I think sometimes you display some asshole tendencies, but you'd cut your arm off before you'd do business with an arms dealer and threaten your own company."

Bennett's chest felt frozen. He just looked at her.

She walked up to him. "People talk. It's what people do. They like to connect dots and make up stupid theories. Social media and the press have just made it worse.

People make judgments on the tiniest things, and they have no patience or intelligence to discover the truth."

"What's the truth here?" he asked.

"That you're the good guy, Mr. Knightley. L'Orage is targeting you, but we will stop him."

Bennett wanted her. So fucking badly. "I'm not always good." Desire vibrated through him.

She smiled. "Oh, I believe that."

He gripped her jaw. "Hadley..."

She closed the distance between them and kissed him.

Fuck.

Need rose up and choked him, gripping him with demanding claws.

He thrust his tongue into her mouth, and her arms slid around his neck. She moaned, her body pressing hard against his.

She moved against him, his cock responding. It was as though both of them were starved for contact.

All his emotion shifted, the anger giving way to hot need.

"I want you," he growled.

She made a sound. "Maybe this is a good idea. To get it out of our system."

Oh, she thought this was a one-shot deal? An itch to scratch?

Bullshit.

He'd enjoy showing her how wrong she was.

Touch and taste Hadley Lockwood just once? No, that was the dumbest thing he'd ever heard.

"You're stressed and upset," she said. "You need to get rid of that so you can focus—"

He gripped her hips. "You're volunteering to offer me some stress relief?"

Her eyes flashed. "I...just wanted to make sure you're all right."

Bennett's chest hitched. Was he getting to her, too? Getting through those rock-solid walls of hers?

For now, he'd give them both what they wanted.

He spun her around so her back was pressed to his front. "I'm going to make you cry out my name, Hadley."

Her breathing quickened. "You can try."

He nipped her ear. "You like challenging me."

"Someone needs to keep you on your toes."

He nipped her again. She squirmed, rubbing her ass against him.

"Bend over my desk," he ordered.

She pulled in a sharp breath. "Giving into those office fantasies, Mr. Knightley?"

"Giving into my Hadley fantasies. Let me have you. Let me give you what you want."

She looked back at him over her shoulder. Desire was alive in her blue eyes. He knew this would be a move toward trusting him.

Then she stepped away. She took two more steps and reached his desk.

There was no submission in her moves, just pure seduction.

Then she pressed her palms to the glossy surface and bent over. Her skirt stretched over her arse.

Bennett's cock was so hard it hurt. He flexed his hands.

He closed the distance and ran one palm over the curve of her buttocks. She made a small sound. He slid the other hand into her hair, pulling it free of its pins.

Desire was pounding hard, his control paper-thin. He gripped the hem of her skirt and pulled it up, baring her gossamer-thin, black-lace panties.

Fuck. He worked hard not to come in his trousers like a teenager.

He smoothed a hand over the lace, then pulled her panties down.

"So damn pretty, Hadley." He slid a hand between her thighs.

She jerked and made a sound.

"I can smell you. So wet." He ran his knuckles through her folds. "I can't wait to taste you."

"Bennett—" She reared up, an edge in her voice.

He gripped the nape of her neck and pinned her to the desk. "It's okay. This is just pleasure. Just feel."

He heard her suck in a breath. Such a beautiful contradiction. She was all skill and confidence in her work, but nervous, if someone got too close.

He stroked her and then slid a finger inside. She moaned.

"Tight and wet for me." He added another finger.

"*Bennett.*" She squirmed.

"Just feel, Hadley." He worked his fingers inside her. His thumb found her clit.

Her breathing was coming in hard, fast pants. "I..."

"What, beautiful? What's scaring you?" He kept up his rhythm, his fingers plunging into her pussy.

She rocked back against him, a cry escaping her. "I'm not afraid. I want to come."

He bent over her, and bit the back of her neck. "Don't lie. There'll be no lies between us."

She made an angry sound, and shoved hard onto his fingers.

"You...you make me want to trust you, dammit. To let go."

Elation filled him. He kept working her, heard a needy sound rip free of her.

"I've got you, Hadley. I promise."

Then Bennett dropped to his knees. He cupped her ass cheeks and parted them enough to get his mouth on her pussy.

Hadley cried out his name.

He licked, lapping at her slick juices. So, so sweet. He stabbed his tongue inside her and used one hand to find her clit.

She struggled, and cried out again.

"Come, beautiful. *Now.*"

She bucked and screamed. He licked her through her violent release, until she slumped on his desk.

Bennett rose. Hell, his knees were weak, and his cock was as hard as steel, throbbing painfully. Looking at a limp Hadley on his desk, her high heels discarded on the floor, and her bare arse on display, didn't help.

"Holy..." She straightened and turned, still breathing hard.

She pushed her skirt down and eyed him, her gaze dropping to the tent in the front of his suit trousers.

Her lips curled. "Now it's my turn."

HADLEY SMOOTHED DOWN HER SKIRT. Her heart was still racing, and little aftershocks of pleasure shivered through her.

He'd taken her over, and she'd let him. She was used to controlling sex. To never fully letting go. She could still feel his hands on her, in her. She let her gaze travel over him. There was fire in his eyes; his face was stark with need.

It soothed something inside her. He wasn't in control. He was as lost as she was.

She saw the way his fists were clenched by his sides. No, not in control at all. The large bulge in his trousers made her belly clench. She'd felt it pushed against her. He'd been blessed in more ways than one.

She took a step toward him. "My turn."

"It's not about turns. I wanted to give you pleasure."

She pressed her hands to his chest and pushed him. He dropped into one of the guest chairs in front of his desk. His gaze was locked on her, unblinking.

"My turn," she murmured again.

Now Hadley dropped to her knees. She saw Bennett stiffen. She pressed her hands to his thighs and felt the rock-hard muscle under his trousers. She skimmed her hands up his legs.

"Hadley—"

"You're going to groan my name, Bennett."

"*Fuck*," he bit out.

She moved her hands to his waist, and unbuckled his belt.

God, the man really was gorgeous. The rugged edge wasn't hidden by his expensive suit or shirt. She slid the zipper down. His gaze didn't move from her face, like he physically couldn't look away.

She found black boxer shorts and pushed them down, freeing his heavy cock.

She made a sound of appreciation. He was thick and hard.

"It should be unfair for a man to possess a billion dollars, a muscled body, *and* a big, beautiful cock."

He let out a strained laugh.

She wrapped her hand around his erection, curling her fingers down to the thick base.

Bennett groaned.

Oh, now that was a sound she liked very much.

Enjoying the silky heat of him, she gave him a squeeze. The head was slick with pre-come, and Hadley really wanted to taste him. Her own arousal flared back to life.

"Hadley?"

She didn't look up from exploring his cock. "Hmm?"

"Put my cock in your mouth and suck me, before I lose my mind."

She looked up, pumping him again, loving the hungry expression on his face. "I'm in charge now."

He growled.

Keeping her gaze locked on his, she lowered her head and licked him.

He made a desperate sound.

The musky taste of him made her shiver. She closed her mouth around him and sucked him deep.

Now his groan turned deep and guttural. "Fuck... *Hadley*."

She sucked harder.

He shifted, and slid both hands into her hair, cupping her head. He didn't force her movements, his fingers just tightened in her hair, like he needed an anchor.

She sucked, lifting her head, then swallowing him back down.

"So good." His words were barely decipherable.

She looked up at him. He was watching her face, his features strained.

She moved faster, drunk on the pleasure she was giving him. His erection was deep in her mouth, and she felt his big body tensing.

With each stroke of his cock in her mouth, she worked her throat and he grunted.

Then his body jerked.

Hadley sucked harder and heard him curse.

He came down her throat, his groan long and deep.

Wow. She swallowed and felt tingles through her body. She liked driving him wild, liked giving him pleasure.

He eased his cock out of her mouth and she licked her lips.

"Damn, Hadley. You destroyed me." He pulled her up and settled her in his lap.

She pressed her face to his warm throat. He smelled so good.

He ran a hand down her arm in a lazy, intimate move.

She swallowed. She didn't usually snuggle. She had nice dinners, good sex, and then she left.

But Bennett Knightley made her want all kinds of things she knew would be bad for her.

"I'm glad you came to check on me," he said.

"And made all your office fantasies come to life."

He chuckled. "I won't lie. It's going to be hard to work in here and not picture you making me come."

She couldn't stop herself from stroking her hand inside his shirt, caressing the strong column of his throat.

For a second, she had the image of him splayed out on a big bed—she was sure he had a big bed—and her stroking him all over. Discovering exactly what he liked.

Panic, sly and sneaky, closed around her throat.

"Come home with me," he said.

Hadley stiffened. "That's very tempting, but I need some sleep, and I have work to do." Plus she needed some space to clear her head.

"Running again, Hadley?"

She met his gaze. "I'm not sure tangling with you is a good idea."

His lips quirked. "You said that before, yet here you are on my lap, with no panties on, I have your taste on my lips, and I just came in that very sexy mouth of yours."

Her belly contracted. "I'm leaving now."

He sighed and loosened his hold. "Okay." He kissed her. It was deep, delicious, and she couldn't stop her small moan as she kissed him back.

When she stood, her knees were a little shaky. She glanced around. "Where's my underwear?"

His smile turned sexy. "I have no idea."

Hadley let out an exasperated breath. "Knightley—"

He rose as well, tucking himself away and fastening his trousers. "I'll see you in the morning, Ms. Lockwood." He reached out, his fingers grazing her jaw.

She felt tingles all over her. He was too close, too tempting. She took a step back. "Good night, Bennett."

She tried to tell herself that she wasn't retreating, but she had to get out of there before she threw her arms around the man and dragged him to the floor.

She made herself walk out the door.

"*Damn.*" Her voice was shaky as she stalked through the quiet office.

She'd always known Bennett was dangerous.

She was only now realizing just how much.

CHAPTER EIGHT

Walking into the Secura office the next day, Hadley refused to admit that she felt much more relaxed.

There was nothing like a world-class orgasm, then watching a big, strong man find his pleasure thanks to you, to loosen you up.

"Morning, Halle." Jack strolled past with a wave.

Hadley waved back. She wasn't quite sure how to play things today with Bennett.

Thanks for making me come on your desk.

No.

Thanks for letting me suck on your big cock.

She snorted.

A man coming out of one of the meeting rooms heard her, and eyed her with surprise.

She shot him a serene smile and kept walking.

Maybe they'd just pretend it didn't happen.

Her stomach roiled. A part of her hated the idea of

him looking at her blank faced, like he'd never touched her.

Another part of her was just plain terrified. Bennett Knightley was getting to places she hadn't let anyone, ever.

She dragged in a breath. She had an arms dealer to catch. That's what she should be focused on.

She turned a corner and saw Bennett standing at Maudie's desk, telling his assistant something.

It was like a punch to the belly. His shirt was tucked into his lean waist. It was white today, which set off his tanned skin. How the hell was he so tanned? He should be pasty white, like all good Brits in the winter.

Her gaze ran over his clean-shaven jaw. The five o'clock shadow would be back by the afternoon. *Oh, God.* Why was he so delicious?

She felt a pulse between her legs. Her gaze dropped to his hand where he was holding a file. She stared at those long fingers. She could still feel them on her, in her...

Suddenly, his head shot up and his gaze locked on hers. He dropped the file on Maudie's desk with a slap and stalked toward Hadley.

"Hey!" Maudie grumbled. "We aren't finished."

Bennett ignored her. "Halle, I need a word."

His fingers wrapped around her arm, and he tugged her toward his office.

One look at his face and all she saw was heat.

He closed the door, then whirled. He backed her against the wall.

Hadley felt her body go up in flames. She slid her hands into his hair and pulled his head to hers.

Their lips collided. They grabbed at each other, mouths messing in a hot wild kiss. Tongues stroked.

Hadley's heart pounded in her ears. Damn, he tasted *so* good.

He eased his thigh between hers and she rubbed against it, moaning into his mouth.

"Dreamed of you," he said against her lips. "Was fucking hard all night, imagining your mouth on my cock."

She undulated against him. She'd dreamed of him too, dammit.

"This morning, lying in my bed, I stroked my cock thinking of you," he said.

She moaned.

"I came hard, wishing you were there."

"*Bennett*," she breathed.

There was a loud knock on the door. "Bennett, your meeting is in five minutes." Maudie's muffled voice came through the wood. "You and Halle need to be there."

Bennett pressed his forehead against Hadley's.

"Duty calls," she said.

He pressed a quick kiss to her lips. "After you, Ms. Lockwood, I mean, Ms. Atwood."

She fixed her skirt, then spotted some lipstick on his lips.

"Hold still." She ran her thumb across his mouth.

His gaze dropped to her lips.

"Bennett."

"Shit, you need to stop touching me."

"You're former SAS. Where's that awesome compartmentalizing?"

"All my compartments are filled with you."

Her chest warmed, but she fought it down. She stepped back, and checked her face in the mirror on his wall.

When they walked into the meeting room, she hoped they didn't look like they'd just been mauling each other.

Soon, they were sucked into work. She felt her phone vibrate and pulled it out to check her messages. It was from Hex.

Bang him yet?

Don't you have work to do?

I can multitask. Well?

No comment.

OMG, you did!

I didn't. Not quite.

So almost. I'm fanning myself.

Get back to work. You need to find a man.

Pfft. They're all annoying.

The meeting finished. A man she didn't recognize came in and whispered something to Bennett. He caught her gaze.

She waited for the room to empty. She thought it was

a little dangerous for them to be in an empty room, alone, with a huge conference table a foot away.

She cleared her throat. "What's wrong?"

"An employee didn't turn up to work today. We can't get in touch with him, and he's not answering his phone." Bennett's face was grim.

She straightened. "Any red flags on this employee?"

Bennett gave a frustrated shake of his head. "Ajay Patel is good at his job. He's part of the IT team. No criminal record. He worked for the Army for a bit, but it didn't suit his creative temperament. As far as I know, the closest he's ever come to being in trouble was at a few climate-change protests. All in all, he's a good employee."

"Okay, send me all his details, and I'll get Hex on the case."

Bennett scraped a hand through his hair. She realized now it was the thing he did when he was most frustrated.

"If he gets hurt..."

And here Bennett was, worrying about the young man first, a man who might be betraying him.

She gripped his arm and squeezed.

Then her phone rang. "It's Hex." She thumbed it and put it on speaker. "Hey, Hex. I'm here with Bennett, and you're on speaker."

"Hadley, Kitty Wentworth is on the move."

Hadley straightened. "Where?"

"She's heading to Shoreditch, but she's supposed to be in a pilates class."

Bennett's gaze narrowed. "Ajay lives in Shoreditch."

"Who's Ajay?" Hex asked.

"A young Secura employee who didn't show for work

today," Hadley told her. "No one can get in touch with him."

"Send me his deets," Hex said.

"I'll bring the car around," Bennett said. "Let's go and see what trouble Kitty's stirring up."

Hadley eyed him. "Surveillance only, Knightley."

He gave a sharp nod.

She'd need to keep an eye on him. She could feel the tension pumping off him. He'd gone into hyperaware battle mode.

"I CAN'T BELIEVE you think a Bentley is a good surveillance car."

Bennett flicked on the indicator and took a corner. "It's a black SUV. No one will give it a second glance."

Hadley snorted. "It's a Bentley Bentayga, Knightley. Of course, people will look."

"Kitty Wentworth won't see us. She's wealthy and a society wife. She's not expecting anyone to be trailing her."

"How did you manage to ditch Henry?" Hadley asked.

"He listens when I give him orders."

Hadley scoffed. "You snuck out."

"Yeah."

After a twenty-minute drive, Bennett pulled onto a Shoreditch street and found a parking space. He turned off the engine, then craned his head to look across the street at the row of terrace houses.

"This is Ajay's place?" she asked.

His jaw was tight. "Yeah, the one with the red door."

Hadley pulled out her phone. "Kitty must be a hell of a lay to seduce all these young men."

He grunted. "She's experienced, and she's taking advantage of naïve, inexperienced people. Hell, I almost didn't hire Ajay because he was so shy and anxious. As far as I know, he's never had a girlfriend."

"That's her car." Hadley nodded at the silver Mercedes across the street. She tapped on her phone. "I'm accessing the bug. We should be in range."

Voices came through the phone.

"Oh, baby, is this all for me?" Kitty's breathless voice. "You're *so* hard."

A low moan sounded.

Hadley pulled a face. "*Ew.*"

"That's it, baby." Kitty made some husky noises. Then came the sounds of slapping skin.

Bennett winced.

Hadley met his gaze and pulled a face. He tried not to laugh.

"I love it from behind. Faster, baby."

Hadley slapped a hand over her face. "There goes doggy style for a while. *Ugh.*"

Bennett leaned over and cupped her jaw. "I bet I could change your mind."

She smiled as the cries coming through the phone increased. "Do not try to be charming and seductive right now, Knightley."

The sex sounds reached a crescendo. Bennett winced again.

"Thanks, baby," Kitty said breathlessly. "I needed that. You are *so* good."

"Kitty." Ajay's voice sounded like he'd just run a marathon. "I love being with you."

Bennett heard the infatuation.

He wanted to strangle Kitty Wentworth.

"Now, are you ready for the job I mentioned?" Kitty asked.

Silence for a beat. "I'm not sure—"

"Baby." The sound of kissing. "This is important. You're doing the right thing. Don't forget that."

"But Secura—"

"Shh. It's going to be fine. You're a warrior." The sound of more kissing. "Wait for my message. Then maybe we can go away somewhere for a while."

"Just the two of us?" Ajay sounded hopeful.

"Yes. You know my husband doesn't treat me well. Ignores me most of the time." More kissing sounds.

"Jesus, she's a real piece of work." Hadley ended the bug connection.

A moment later, Kitty bounced out of the house, fixing her hair. She looked like she didn't have a trouble in the world.

Bennett gripped the wheel, keeping his gaze locked on the woman.

Kitty slipped into her Mercedes and pulled away.

He just stared at Ajay's building. How had the young man gotten sucked into this?

Bennett blew out a breath.

"We need to put Ajay under surveillance," Hadley said.

With a nod, Bennett reached for his phone. "I'll have Henry organize it."

Hadley's phone rang and she held up a finger.

"Hello?" She straightened. "Thanks for calling me back. Really? That's great. No, I can come to you. Where?" A pause. "A-ha. Okay. I'll see you then." She ended the call and smiled.

"Who was that?" he asked.

"That was a string I pulled, that finally paid off. Someone who knows L'Orage."

Bennett sat up straighter. "And is willing to talk to us about him?"

"Yes." Her smile widened. "I'll go and—"

"I'm coming."

She frowned. "Bennett..."

"I'm coming." He started the engine. "Where are we headed?"

"If you scare him off, or intimidate him—"

"I'll be a good boy, but I'm not letting you go alone to see an associate of L'Orage."

"He's not an associate, and you do know I can defend myself?"

"Yes. I'm still not letting you go alone."

She shook her head. "Fine. Oxford."

He pulled out. "That'll be just over an hour's drive. I'll have to tell Maudie we won't be back for a bit." He winced at that. "Where in Oxford, exactly?"

"The Bodleian Library."

"Who is this guy?"

"We'll find out soon."

CHAPTER NINE

I t was easy to love Oxford.

Hadley looked out the window, taking in the historic buildings. The place had a sense of stately elegance. She wasn't able to fully relax and take in the view, however. She drummed her nails on the dash impatiently. She really hoped this contact could shed some light on L'Orage.

She'd often speculated the two had been in contact. When she'd been with MI6, she'd intercepted some messages between them, but had never proved a link.

And Professor Simon Dummat had refused to talk to her. Until now.

"You're going to put a hole in my Bentley."

She stopped drumming, and looked at Bennett. He drove well, and she had to admit the Bentayga was a smooth ride.

"I just don't want this to be a dead end," she said.

"Me too. I'm still trying to stop myself from going after Kitty bloody Wentworth."

"Henry's watching Ajay?" she asked.

"Yes. Hopefully we can keep him out of trouble, then I'll get him some help."

Of course, he would.

She looked out the windshield. "There's the Bodleian."

The Bodleian was the main research library for the university and one of the oldest libraries in Europe. It was made of several historic buildings. The Radcliffe Camera, a round, domed structure, caught her eye.

Bennett found a parking space a street away, and they headed into the main library, passing through old, arched doors.

Hadley felt as though she was entering a church. The building had a hushed, reverent atmosphere.

"He said he'd be in the Upper Reading Rooms," she whispered.

They headed up the stairs.

A sense of age and learning washed over her. She took in the bookshelves, packed full of books, the students and scholars working at rows of long desks.

They approached a table where an older man in a tweed suit was sitting. He looked to be in his early seventies, with thinning, white hair, and a long, narrow face. He had several books open in front of him, and a cup of tea sat at his elbow.

"Professor Dummat?" she asked.

His head lifted. His gray eyes held a sharp intelligence, and a friendly smile crossed his lips.

"Ah, Ms. Lockwood, I presume." His gaze shifted to Bennett. "And I see you brought company."

"Professor, this is Mr. Bennett—"

"Bennett Knightley. I've seen you in the media, Mr. Knightley. Sit, please."

They sat across the table from the man. Hadley had the vague feeling like she'd been summoned to the principal's office.

"Thank you for speaking with us," she said.

"I was surprised when you contacted me again. But I felt it was time to talk."

"You know L'Orage."

He gave them a faint smile. "Straight to the point."

He didn't say anything else.

"You're a professor here?" Bennett said, but Hadley sensed his impatience. He wasn't interested in small talk.

"I was. I'm retired." He rested his gnarled hands on the table. "But they still invite me back for the odd guest lecture. I was a professor of politics. An ongoing and fascinating subject."

"If you say so," Bennett said.

Dummat smiled. "You were in the military, Mr. Knightley."

"Special forces."

"Ah. You're used to finding the best path forward, and acting quickly and decisively. The opposite of politics."

"Yes."

"How did you meet L'Orage, Professor?" Hadley asked.

The man leaned back. "I ran an online forum for my students to discuss politics and world issues. No subject was taboo. We argued the merit and harm of everything. Oliver turned up in there one day."

Her heart hit her ribs. "Oliver?" she asked.

"He didn't go by L'Orage in his regular life."

Professor Dummat's gaze turned inward. "He was intelligent, asked good questions. Provocative questions. I knew he wasn't a student, but he added a lot to the discussions. He was an anarchist at heart, but conflicted."

"He sells weapons to bastards who murder and kill," Bennett clipped.

Hadley put a hand on his arm. He blew out a breath.

"I don't dispute that Oliver did terrible things." Dummat sipped his tea. "We communicated, engaged in spirited debate, and over time we became friends. I finally worked out who he was." The professor sighed. "There are so many shades of gray in the world. We all have things we regret." His gaze rested on Hadley, then shifted to Bennett. "I assume you both understand that."

"We both served our country, Professor," Bennett said. "So don't go comparing us to L'Orage."

"That wasn't my intention. All I mean is that Oliver had regrets. But it doesn't matter now."

"Doesn't matter—?" Bennett leaned in.

"Bennett." She grabbed his hand and stroked a thumb across his palm.

She met his gaze, and his stayed locked on hers, then he sat back in his seat. She watched him lock all his emotions down and got a glimpse of the soldier in him.

"Professor, unfortunately L'Orage has returned," she said. "He's reactivated old contacts, and he's targeting

Mr. Knightley's company, Secura. He's stealing vital gear and selling it to terrorists."

Dummat's eyes widened. "That's impossible."

"I'm afraid not," she said.

"Your buddy came out of retirement and is fucking with my company," Bennett clipped out. "He's destroying lives."

Dummat set his cup down.

Bennett rose and thumped his fist on the table. The cup rattled, and people nearby glanced over.

"Bennett, sit down, or wait in the car," Hadley said. She wanted to hug him. Jeez, and she was so not a hugger, but she couldn't let him ruin this.

He sat, but he looked stiff.

Hadley leaned forward. "Bennett is understandably angry."

"I understand, I do." Dummat met their gazes. "It's impossible that L'Orage is causing your problems because he's dead."

A hard ball filled Hadley's chest. "You're sure?"

"Very. He had cancer, and so few people he trusted. I flew to Portugal a year ago to be with him. I was there when he died."

There was true grief on the professor's face.

The man's words echoed in her head. *L'Orage was dead.*

"He respected you a lot, Ms. Lockwood. Not just because he appreciated beautiful things. You were dogged, relentless. You almost caught him several times."

"I know. He killed a colleague of mine to escape us."

Sympathy flashed in the older man's eyes.

"He's really dead?" she asked.

The man nodded.

"So who is stealing goods from Secura?" Bennett said icily.

"That is a compelling question," the professor said. "There are many people who are unhappy with us providing military assistance to other countries, and interfering where they feel we shouldn't. Whoever this is, they are clearly using L'Orage's name for a reason."

Pieces started shifting in Hadley's head. "We'd assumed it was L'Orage, so that influenced everything. They wanted his contacts."

"That is likely," Dummat agreed.

She nodded. "He could literally pick up where L'Orage left off, with buyers all over the world."

"Buyers willing to purchase stolen goods," Bennett said.

"There are avenues and leads we haven't looked at because we assumed it was L'Orage." She met Bennett's gaze. "This helps, Bennett."

He raised a hand scraped it through his hair. "It feels like another dead end."

God, he looked frustrated. She wanted to hug him again.

She stirred. "Thank you, Professor Dummat."

The older man nodded. "I wish you luck tracking down your foe." He glanced at Bennett. "Your company does good work, Mr. Knightley. I hope this is sorted out soon."

Bennett stood too and gave the man a nod.

As they headed out of the library, Hadley kept glancing at Bennett. "Are you all right?"

"No."

She took his hand.

His fingers gripped hers, tangling them together. He didn't seem inclined to let her go.

"You look like you need to hit the gym, or spar with Henry." Release some of the dangerous buildup.

"I'm not going to lose it."

But there was a muscle ticking relentlessly in his jaw. She reached up and touched it. His gaze sliced to hers.

"What do you need?" she asked quietly.

"I suppose a hot quickie in the Bentley isn't an option."

She shot him a look.

He blew out a breath. "Come on. I know a place we can visit that always lowers my blood pressure."

BENNETT TOOK the bend in the country road and heard Hadley hiss.

He glanced over and saw her gripping the door.

"I forgot how narrow country lanes are here," she grumbled. "And the hedges are so close that you can't see a damn thing."

"Don't you trust my driving?" he asked.

"I don't trust the *other* people driving."

He pulled over to the side to let a car pass. Bushes scratched along the side of the car.

"Where are we going?" she asked.

"You'll see."

They were just outside Oxford. They'd passed through several tiny villages.

Hadley sighed. "Even at the end of winter, the countryside is beautiful."

The lane turned, twisting through lots of trees that arched overhead, covering it like a tunnel. Right now, they were missing their leaves, but come spring, they'd be bursting with green. The fields would fill with wildflowers.

Then he slowed and pulled through a rustic stone gateway.

"What is this?" Hadley leaned forward. "A farm?"

"Yes."

"Whose farm?"

"My parents."

Her mouth opened, closed. "Your parents? You're taking me to meet your parents?"

"You said to do something so I could get a grip on things." Anger was still a low hum in his blood. "Sitting in my mother's kitchen, eating whatever she's baked today, always does the trick."

Hadley's mouth flattened into a line.

"Not everything Mum bakes is good. She can be a bit hit or miss." He winked. "Don't tell her I said that though, or I'll deny it. And my father fancies himself a farmer. He has some sheep, and an orchard. Don't get him started on his goats and making goat cheese, though."

"Bennett—"

"Here we are." The house came into view.

It was a rambling cottage, made of natural stone and

wood. In the summer, the garden was lush and filled with flowers. His mum was better with plants than most of her kitchen pursuits.

"My parents moved here after they retired." Bennett had bought the farm for them. "Dad was career Army, Mum was a schoolteacher. High school. She wields that teacher voice like a pro."

"You're close to them."

There was a wistful note buried deep in her voice. "Yeah. You're not close to yours?"

She made a scoffing noise. "They aren't the worst people in the world."

"Not a ringing endorsement."

"They're classic high society. Polished, aloof, and live for keeping up appearances. My father generally boinks his young personal assistants, but my mother is more eclectic in her tastes. She alternates from young toy boys to older, distinguished lovers. They're discreet, of course. Neither of them are vulgar enough to flaunt their affairs in public, or worse, get a divorce."

Bennett stared at her. Hell, no wonder Hadley didn't trust anyone. She had bad examples at home, then some dickhead agent had taken a hammer to her already fragile trust.

"Don't look at me like that," she said. "My parents are more the norm than yours."

He pulled the SUV to a stop. "I don't believe that."

She straightened. "All right, let's get this over with."

The front door of the house opened, and his parents appeared.

His dad might like to putter around the farm, but he

still looked like the military man he'd been. Michael Knightley was fit, with a straight bearing, and gray hair clipped short. Bennett's mother was shorter, softer, with a handsome face, and dark-brown hair she kept dyed. Patty Knightley had no interest in surrendering to her grays.

"Bennett! What a lovely surprise." His mother hurried forward.

Hadley slid out of the car and his mother did a double take.

"You brought a woman," she breathed, like he'd brought the Hope diamond.

"Mum, don't embarrass me."

His mother ignored him and went straight to Hadley. She took both of Hadley's hands, cradling them in hers.

"I'm Patty, and this is Michael."

Bennett's father was eyeing Hadley with a critical look. His dad always worried about the glossy, frivolous gold diggers Bennett often attracted since Secura had become a success.

"Mum, Dad, this is Hadley Lockwood."

She shot him a look about not using her alias. Then she found a smile. "It's a pleasure."

"How do you know Bennett?" his mother asked.

"Well..." Hadley glanced his way. "We kind of work together."

His dad's brows snapped together. "You work for Secura?"

"Temporarily," she said.

Bennett stepped up beside her. "Want to get out the rubber hose, Dad?"

"I'm just asking questions," his father said. "Politely."

Bennett scoffed. "Hadley's working undercover at Secura to find the fucker who's stealing my fucking gear."

"Undercover?" His dad's eyes widened.

"Bennett, no cursing," his mother admonished.

"Mum, you curse. And Dad curses all the time."

She glared at him. "Don't make us look bad in front of Hadley."

"Undercover?" Bennett's dad said, again.

"Come in," his mum said. "I'll pop the kettle on. And I made some scones this morning."

Phew. His mother's scones were generally good.

They moved inside. The house had refinished wooden floors and fresh, white walls with beams overhead. The kitchen was in a new extension at the back of the cottage, and was big and airy. The place had a cozy feel, and copper pots hung, gleaming, above the stove. His mother had whacked him on the arse with one when he'd trampled her prized primroses in the garden when he was thirteen. It still had the dent in the side.

The kitchen also had a lovely view of the farm out the wide windows.

His mum bustled around, filling the copper kettle with water and setting it on the stove. His dad leaned against an island with a butcher-block top.

"So, what makes you qualified to be undercover, Hadley?" Bennett's dad asked. "You a cop?"

"Dad, you're like a bloody dog with a bone," Bennett said.

"I work in private security," Hadley answered. "For Sentinel Security in New York."

"New York?" His mum looked stricken, no doubt her dreams of a summer wedding dimming.

"Yes, but my family is here," Hadley said. "In London."

"So you visit often?" His mum's face brightened.

"Occasionally. We're not that...close."

"Lockwood." Bennett's father nodded. "Baron Astley and Lady Lockwood?"

"That's them."

"And what's your background to be working security?" his dad continued.

"Jeez, Dad." Bennett grabbed a scone off the plate on the table, and slathered it with jam and cream.

"I started my career at MI6," Hadley said.

"A spook?" His father looked reluctantly impressed.

The kettle whistled. Bennett's mum waved her hands. "Everyone, sit down at the table."

They sat at the long, rustic farm table, and his mum enjoyed fussing around them. Soon they were all eating and drinking.

"You have a lovely home, Mrs. Knightly," Hadley said.

"Thank you. Bennett bought it for us. We love it here, although I sometimes miss the house where we raised all the kids." She smiled. "The boys were always playing pranks on each other, and driving their sister crazy."

Hadley eyed Bennett. "Pranks, huh?"

"I've matured."

His dad made a sound. "They still play pranks on each other."

His mum rolled her eyes. "They do. Never grew out of it."

"So, some more shipments are missing?" his dad asked.

Anger fired in Bennett's gut. "Yes. And we have a mole at Secura who's leaking the information."

"Shit," his dad said.

"Michael!" his mother squawked.

"Not sure how many." Bennett thought about the intel the professor had given them. "Or who's behind it."

He felt a hand on his arm and looked at Hadley. She squeezed his bicep.

It eased some of the turbulence and he nodded at her.

When he looked back, his mother was beaming at them.

They chatted some more, and he slid an arm along the back of Hadley's chair. He liked seeing her here, charming his parents.

And he realized he did feel better. She'd been right to make him come here.

Hadley's cell phone rang. "Excuse me, I need to take this." She rose, walking toward the hall. "Hex?"

"We approve." His mother's smile was wide.

"Mum—"

"Don't pretend with me, Bennett Knightley. I see the way you look at her."

Was he that obvious?

His mum grabbed his hand. "I know things haven't been easy for you since you left the military. I know you've been hurting."

"Mum—"

"I'm your mother. If my child is hurting, I hurt."

He met her warm gaze. "I love you."

She smiled. "I know you do. And we love you too. You deserve love, Bennett, no matter where you've been or what you've done. You deserve her."

His heart gave a good kick against his ribs.

Hadley returned, her face serious. "I'm sorry, but we need to get back to London."

He nodded and rose. He kept his voice low. "What happened?"

"Kitty just made plans for a meeting at a play at the Countess Theatre tonight. She used some kind of code words, and Hex suspects that L'Orage, or whoever is pretending to be him, might be there."

Bennett's heart thumped. This was it. They could catch the fucker. "Let's go."

She nodded and looked around him. "Thanks again, Mr. and Mrs. Knightley."

"Michael and Patty." His mother hugged Hadley. "Take care of him for us."

Hadley blinked, then nodded. "I'll give you some privacy." She headed out the front door.

"We really like her, my darling."

"I could tell, Mum."

His dad clapped a hand to his shoulder. "Don't fuck it up, son."

"Thanks, Dad."

They reached the front door just in time to see Hadley whirl and flip a man dressed all in black over her shoulder. The man landed flat on his back on the gravel driveway beside the Bentley. Hadley pressed her boot to the man's throat.

"He was skulking around. I saw him close the hood—er, bonnet. He did something to the vehicle."

Bennett hurried forward.

"Fuck me," the man on the ground groaned.

"Brandon?" Bennett's mother said with a gasp.

Bennett strolled over and grinned. "You idiot."

Hadley blinked. "You know him?"

"I'm related to him. He's my brother."

"Oh." She lifted her boot.

Bennett's brother rose, rubbing his side and dusting himself off.

"Brandon Michael Knightley, what did you think you were doing?" Bennett's mum snapped.

"I was just messing with Ben's fancy car." He rubbed the back of his neck. He was two inches shorter than Bennett, with a leaner build.

Bennett shook his head.

"I didn't expect Wonder Woman to appear." Brandon looked at Hadley, and his eyes widened. "She looks a bit like Wonder Woman."

Bennett didn't like the way his brother was looking at her. He wrapped an arm around her shoulders. "Mine."

Hadley shot him a glare before looking back at his brother. "Sorry about that."

"Oh, no worries," Brandon said with a growing smile. "Nothing's broken."

"Bennett and Hadley need to get back to London. You, inside." Their mother pointed toward the house.

"Bennett, your father will fix whatever your brother did to your SUV. Hadley, please come back."

Hadley smiled.

Bennett squeezed her shoulders. "Let's go catch a bad guy."

They slid into the Bentley while Bennett's father opened the bonnet. She turned in her seat. "I have an important job to do as soon as we get back to the city."

Bennett raised a brow.

"I need you to drop me at Regent Street. I have to go shopping for a dress to wear to the theatre."

"You're going to go shopping?"

"We have to blend in, Knightley. This is *very* important."

CHAPTER TEN

B ennett drove his Ferrari Roma over the Vauxhall Bridge, heading to the St. George's Wharf to pick up Hadley.

She'd gone bloody shopping. And looked happy about it too. He shook his head. Clothes shopping was one of those necessary evils, in his opinion.

Now, if he could convince Hadley to hang around, he'd happily let her do all his shopping.

His gaze fell on the MI6 building. That place had helped form that hard shell of hers. Watching her bemused look at his parents, at a normal, loving family, had made him angry at Hadley's own parents. How could they have a daughter as amazing as Hadley, and not shower her with affection?

Bennett shook his head. He needed to get his mind off Hadley and think about tonight.

They might actually catch whoever was masquerading as L'Orage. He frowned, turning onto the street leading to her place. So far, this investigation was just throwing up more questions.

He pulled up outside Hadley's building, and noted a few people eyeing his sweet red Ferrari. He loved the car, but he only drove it for special occasions, since it garnered so much attention.

Tonight, he needed to look the part.

They were heading into the West End to the Countess Theatre. He'd been there once for a tortuous play with his sister.

The doors of the building opened and all the air clogged in his lungs.

Fuck.

He opened his door and stood, never taking his gaze off Hadley.

The dress was black, but that seemed such a plain description for something so dazzling.

The V-neck showed lots of skin, and there were cutouts on each side showing more skin. It hugged her hips and arse before flaring out around her feet, making him think of a mermaid. Her hair was loose, all silky and sleek. She didn't wear a necklace to interrupt the smooth skin, but she had small diamond studs in her ears, and a cuff of diamonds around one slender wrist.

She was holding a silky looking black coat in one hand.

Her gaze skimmed over his tuxedo, appreciation flaring in her eyes.

He strode to meet her.

"Nice car," she said.

"You should be wearing the coat. It's cold."

"I wanted you to get the full effect of the dress."

"Oh, I got it." He took her coat and held it up.

She turned and Bennett groaned.

"Seriously?" There was no back.

She glanced over one slim shoulder and smiled. "You should see what's under the dress."

He groaned again.

"I see my shopping trip paid off," she said smugly.

He wanted to run his lips over her bare back, trace down her spine.

She slipped into the coat and wrapped it around her. He held the car door open for her, and she sank into the passenger seat.

Bennett circled the car and got in. He didn't start the engine. Instead, he pulled a small box out of his pocket. "I got you something."

Her eyes narrowed. "Bennett, I don't need gifts."

"You said it's important we blend in and look the part. This will help do that."

She huffed out a breath.

He opened the box.

Her lips parted. The long dangle of earrings were made of a mix of diamonds—white, blue, and pink. "They're stunning, but too much, Bennett."

He wanted to see her wearing them. "A loan, then." He had no intention of taking them back.

She hesitated, then took the earrings. It only took her a moment to swap out her studs for the pretty earrings. They looked beautiful on her.

Well satisfied, he smiled and started the engine.

"No more gifts after this. Umbrellas and chocolates are one thing, diamond earrings are something else."

"Sure."

She eyed him suspiciously.

Bennett revved the engine and set off for the West End.

"So, we watch Kitty and see who she meets with," Hadley said.

"Yes." His hands flexed on the wheel. "I want to catch this bastard. I want this to be over."

"So keen to be rid of me?"

He glanced at her. "No."

Their gazes met.

She tucked some hair behind her ear. "Whoever is doing this, it isn't L'Orage."

"No."

"So who is it?"

"If I knew that, I'd be less pissed because they'd be behind bars." Or dead if he got his hands on them.

"Since I stopped running everything through L'Orage's usual MO, I've been thinking," she said.

"Go on."

"This is all focused on Secura."

Bennett frowned. "We knew that already."

"And Secura is you."

"What are you getting at?"

"This is personal, Knightley. Someone is targeting you."

He made a scoffing sound. "They want the goods Secura makes, and are maybe angling to get their hands on the classified MI6 projects."

"I don't think so. Better vests, boots, uniforms, and even exosuits are important, but not that important."

"I beg to differ."

"In the long-term, yes, but whoever is doing this is out to hurt you now."

Fucking hell. He stared at the car ahead of them. She might have a point.

"So who has an axe to grind with Bennett Knightley?" she asked.

"If you're asking if I have enemies, sure, there'd be some."

"List them for me."

He sighed, breaking as the traffic thickened. "A few business rivals. Falco Inc. and Warden Industries. But I can't see either of those companies doing this. Falco is owned by Dean Blackwell, who is old-school, a gentleman. And Richard and Catherine Trent, the owners of Warden, are too busy digging their company out of financial trouble."

"Because Secura has taken business away from them."

He smiled. "My gear is better."

"Who else? Jilted girlfriends, jealous husbands?"

Bennett scowled. "No girlfriends, and I don't sleep with married women." He stared through the windshield. "I probably made some enemies from my time in the military. But they'd all be in Afghanistan, and they shouldn't know who I am."

She crossed her legs. "I'll send the info to Hex. She's good at digging, so we'll see if anything pings."

"Kitty is our best lead."

"Yes."

They had to get it right tonight.

"Killian has brought in another Sentinel Security member, Bram O'Donovan. They'll both be there tonight. We won't see them unless we need them."

Bennett sure as hell wouldn't turn down help from Killian Hawke.

They reached the Countess Theatre, and traffic slowed to a crawl. The sidewalks were filled with people out for an evening of fun.

Bennett pulled up in front of the old building, noting that there were some paparazzi snapping shots of people entering the theatre.

He stepped out of the car, and flashes erupted.

"Knightley, who's your date?" someone called out.

"Knightley, this way." Shutter snaps filled the air.

He ignored them and helped Hadley out of the car. More flashes exploded. She expertly kept her head lowered and face obscured.

Henry emerged from the crowd and took Bennett's keys.

"Hi, Henry," Hadley said.

"You look nice." He glanced at Bennett. "You're fucked."

Bennett nodded at his friend. "Thanks for the pep talk."

He took Hadley's arm and led her inside. The lobby was crowded with people sipping drinks. He took her coat and checked it. He couldn't stop his gaze wandering over her bare shoulders.

Hadley cast a discreet scan across the crowd. "I don't see our friend."

"Let's get to our seats. We'll have a good view from there."

He led her up the curved stairs, nodding hellos to people, but not stopping.

He led Hadley into a small private box.

"Oh, this is nice," she said.

They were shrouded in darkness in the box, but had an excellent view of not only the stage, but the tiers of seats below.

A few people were already seated, but most of the seats were still empty.

Bennett sat, and took a few breaths. Anticipation was winging through him, like it always did right before a mission.

He really wanted to find this bastard. Desperately.

Hadley took his hand. "We've got this."

We. Shit, he liked hearing that. He liked working with Hadley, liked watching her, liked touching her.

He wanted more. So much more that he knew he'd scare her.

He needed to treat Hadley like a mission as well. One step at a time, don't move too quickly or give away your position.

And he was a man who had a very high mission success rate.

———

SHE COULDN'T COMPLAIN about the seats.

The plush, private box had a very good view. Hadley arched forward a little, looking down across the theatre. Kitty wouldn't be able to see them in the shadows, but they should be able to see her.

Hadley felt a fine tension from Bennett. He was preternaturally still, watching the crowd below like a hawk.

She was sure that he'd been like this with his SAS team. Hiding in the shadows, waiting to achieve his mission objective.

More people started filtering in to find their seats.

"Do you see her yet?" Hadley asked.

"Not yet."

She turned her head. "Are you okay?"

His hand resting on his thigh flexed. "Yes." He shifted, and pressed a hand over her thigh. It burned through the silk of her dress. "We're going to end this."

She stared ahead, trying to control the butterflies in her belly. She never got butterflies. This man made her senses go haywire. He was getting under her skin and it scared her.

Her phone dinged. She pulled it out and smiled. It was another email from Gabbi. In the attached picture, Cora was in a pink ballet tutu that Hadley had given her, posing with her arms above her head.

"Who's that?"

Hadley glanced at him. Bennett was unabashedly looking at her phone.

"No one," she said.

"Really?" He arched a brow.

She sighed. "Her name is Cora."

"And who is Cora?"

She hesitated. "She's a little girl staying at a domestic violence shelter in New York." She smiled. "Nightingale House does amazing work. Giving shelter and other support to women who've suffered partner violence."

He studied her face. "Women who'd been let down by the people who should protect them."

Hadley lifted her chin. "Yes."

"And you volunteer there."

"When I can."

He stroked her jaw. "You are a remarkable woman, Hadley."

She made a scoffing sound. "Hardly. What I do isn't enough. There are so many women, so many children, who need safety and security."

She had to look away from his penetrating stare. Then his fingers tightened.

She glanced back. "Bennett?"

"There she is."

Hadley looked down. Kitty Wentworth wore an elegant, dove-gray dress, with beading that shimmered under the lights. She was holding the arm of her husband. It didn't look like a marriage in trouble to Hadley.

Did Ian Wentworth know about his wife's extracurricular activities? Did he care?

Maybe the Wentworths were like Hadley's parents. Did their own things, including taking lovers when it suited them.

Still, Hadley guessed having ties to the prime minister, Ian Wentworth wouldn't like any sort of link to terrorist activity.

Kitty and her husband took their seats. Bennett watched the couple, his face intense.

"When she gets up, we follow," Hadley said.

He nodded.

Then Hadley saw another couple enter the theatre, and groaned.

"What?" Bennett asked.

"My parents." She'd have to be careful not to let them see her.

Bennett leaned forward, and his gaze zeroed in on her parents walking to their seats.

"You look like your mother, but have your father's height."

"That's all I got from them, thankfully."

People were greeting her parents. She saw her mother icily say hello to one woman, before spying another woman and pouring on an effusive welcome. She lavished attention on her favorites, and poured ice on the people she felt beneath her. She'd done the same to her children.

Her father just looked bored.

Bennett cleared his throat. "They seem..."

"Cold," she said. "I used to wonder if they had ice in their veins. They only care about themselves."

"Where did you spring from, then? You're the total opposite to that."

She couldn't stop her smile. The praise felt nice. "I was pretty sure I was adopted when I was a child. Or at least that's what I tried to tell myself. That someone left me on their doorstep."

Bennett leaned closer. "You're an incredible woman,

Hadley. Who contributed to our DNA has very little influence on what we choose to do in life, who we really are inside."

She just stared at him.

Then the lights dimmed, and a spotlight illuminated an actor standing on the stage.

As the show began, Hadley alternated between keeping an eye on the stage, and on Kitty. The woman appeared to be enjoying the play, and didn't look like she was moving before intermission.

Bennett hadn't moved his hand. It still rested on Hadley's thigh, his thumb rubbing distracting circles on her leg through the silk.

A part of her was terrified to let him any closer, but a part of her wanted him touching her skin. She let out a slow breath.

She was in the middle of a mission. She should be focused.

Bennett's hand moved to the slit in her dress, and then his fingers brushed skin. She squirmed.

"Like that?" he whispered.

"*Bennett.*"

He kept rubbing those maddening circles on her skin.

For a second, Hadley let herself absorb the pleasure of his touch and shivered. God, when had a man made her shiver from such a small caress?

The actors on stage were a blur, their voices a drone in her ears.

He didn't move his hand, but his fingers kept up that lazy stroking.

"I like touching you," he murmured in the darkness.

Hadley always kept such a tight leash on herself—on her emotions, her decisions, her wants and needs.

She never trusted anyone enough to truly let go.

What would it feel like? To let everything she felt free?

There was another voice in her head telling her that no one, especially a man, could be trusted with that.

She looked at Bennett's shadowed face. The dips and grooves of his rugged features.

Then she dropped her hand to his strong wrist. His fingers stilled.

Then she pulled his hand higher.

His fingers brushed the lace at her upper thigh, then she heard his swift inhale of breath.

"Hadley. Fuck. What the hell sort of thing are you wearing?" He stroked, feeling the sheer lace of the body-suit she wore.

He nudged it aside and touched the slick flesh between her legs.

She jolted, and tried to stay quiet. She bit down on her lip.

No one else could see what he was doing to her.

"So naughty, wearing something like this," he whispered. "Hell, now I want to know exactly what it looks like."

A small puff of air escaped her. His clever fingers felt so good.

"So wet," he murmured. "I can smell how turned on you are, beautiful."

Two of his fingers delved inside her.

"Bennett." *Oh, God.* She was panting, soft sounds shuddering out of her.

He moved slowly, teasing around her clit. She swallowed a moan.

Then she reached out and gripped his arm. She was on fire, her belly gnawing at her. She felt so needy, empty.

His thick fingers kept invading her and his thumb flicked her clit.

Hadley couldn't hold back a groan of pleasure. She heard Bennett's low, husky laugh.

"I like hearing that sound," he said. "I like knowing that I can make you feel so much."

She shifted her hips to meet the thrust of his fingers. She felt her orgasm building.

She *needed* it.

Her nails bit into his arm. *"Bennett."*

"Come for me, beautiful. Give it to me."

Pleasure swamped her. It felt like fireworks going off inside her, and she bit her lip to stifle her cry. Her body shook, and then his mouth was taking hers, swallowing any noise she made.

Her mind went blank; all her thoughts were on him, and the intense pleasure.

Slowly, reality seeped back in.

She opened her eyes and met his hazel ones. He smiled, his fingers still inside her. Her legs felt weak, and warmth filled her belly.

"Beautiful." He pulled his fingers free and she bit her lip again.

Then he brought his hand to his mouth, putting his

fingers between his lips and licking them clean, making a humming noise.

Her womb contracted.

"You should come with a warning," she said huskily.

His grin flashed again.

Then the lights in the theatre rose. She blinked.

"It's intermission," he said.

They looked down, and saw Kitty and her husband rise with some of the guests.

"We need to get down there," she said.

He nodded. "Let's go."

CHAPTER ELEVEN

I t was a bit of a surprise to realize it was hard to push the feel and sound of what he'd just done to Hadley from his head and focus.

He'd never had that problem in the military. He'd been known for being laser-focused. No woman had tempted him this much.

He followed Hadley down the wide, curved staircase. His gaze ran over her bare shoulders, delicate shoulder blades, and the way the dress clung to her.

She didn't seem to have trouble putting it out of her head. His gut clenched. Damn, maybe she didn't feel this insane attraction to the same level as him? Maybe she really could get him out of her system.

At the bottom of the stairs, she paused and met his gaze. Residual heat burned in her blue eyes.

Relief hit his gut like a punch. *Scratch that.* She felt the same.

The tension in him eased. He took her arm and led her into the crowd.

"Do you see her?" he murmured.

"No." Hadley arched her head. "Her husband is near the bar. But no sign of her."

"Dammit," Bennett muttered.

They moved past Kitty's husband. Bennett looked carefully at all the guests.

"She's not here," he said.

"Come on." Hadley tugged him through a door and into a side corridor. It was wide, with red carpeting and elegant artwork. The restrooms were at one end, and only a few guests were milling around. They moved away from the guests, and Hadley pulled out her phone and tapped.

"I've got her." Hadley tilted the screen to show the glowing dot of the tracker. "She's up one level. Come on."

They headed back to the stairs. At the top, there were many guests, talking, flirting, laughing. But no sign of Kitty. The tinkling of fake laughter was grating.

"This way," Hadley said.

They neared some of the private boxes on the opposite side of the theatre to Bennett's. That's when he heard Kitty's voice.

"Quickly, come with me, Ajay. My husband's here, and he can't catch us."

Fuck. Kitty and Ajay were coming this way.

Hadley spun Bennett. His back hit the wall, then she cupped his cheek and kissed him.

He took over, and turned them so she was trapped between him and the wall. She moaned, and he kept kissing her, only dimly aware of someone passing by.

Then Hadley tapped his arm. He pulled back,

nipping her plump bottom lip. He liked that she looked a little dazed.

She glanced sideways. "Target acquired."

Bennett saw Kitty with Ajay. The young man had thick, black hair and brown skin, and was wearing an ill-fitting suit. Damn, the young, stupid idiot. Bennett watched as Kitty stroked the man's arm, and Ajay's answering look of infatuation.

The couple disappeared down the stairs. Bennett grabbed Hadley's hand and they followed. She smiled like they were just another couple out enjoying the night.

He liked it. He wanted her on his damn arm all the time. Wanted her smiling at him, glaring at him, rolling her eyes at him every day.

They reached the crowded lobby.

"Across the room," she murmured. "Heading into the corridor."

They followed, careful not to move too fast. When they slipped into the corridor, Bennett saw Kitty disappear around the corner.

They picked up speed, and then Hadley pressed her back to the wall and peeked around the corner.

"They've stopped," Hadley murmured. "Kitty's pulled something, a backpack, out of a side room."

"Any sign of L'Orage?" Bennett asked.

Hadley shook her head. "It's just the two of them. Ew. They're kissing."

Bennett gritted his teeth.

"Now they're splitting up. *Dammit*. Ajay's heading in through another door, and Kitty's coming back this way. I'll follow Ajay, you detain Kitty." Hadley pulled out her phone. "Killian, close in."

Bennett and Hadley moved back into the crowded lobby. Kitty and Ajay entered and were swallowed by the crowd. Bennett spotted the sparkle of a woman's dress.

"Got her."

"Crap," Hadley said. "Ajay's heading for the stairs."

"What the hell is he doing?" Bennett said.

"Go. You get Kitty, I'll stop him."

Bennett pushed forward. Kitty was heading back toward her husband, a smug smile on her face.

The bitch.

There was a commotion. He glanced over and saw Ajay running for the stairs. Hadley was chasing after him. There were cries and cursing from the crowd, people stumbling to get out of their way.

Bennett desperately wanted to go with her.

He turned his head and Kitty caught his gaze, her face paling.

Yes, you're busted.

He closed the distance between them.

She schooled her face. "It's Mr. Knightley, right? I—"

"You know exactly who I am. And I know what you are and what you've been doing." He took her arm.

"Sir, let me go," Kitty said with a gasp.

"Come quietly," he said.

"I don't think so." She raised her voice. "Let me go. You're hurting me!"

Heads turned.

"Kitty, you're done. You're going to jail for a long time."

There was a flash of fear before she hid it with bravado. "No, I'm Lady Kitty Wentworth. I have coffee every week with the wife of the prime minister."

"That's not going to save you."

"What's going on?" Kitty's husband arrived. "Release my wife."

"Your wife is working with a known arms dealer who supplies terrorists."

There were gasps from the people nearby. Ian Wentworth's face darkened.

"And she's been seducing young men for intel," Bennett added.

Now Ian Wentworth's face turned red.

Kitty gasped. "How *dare* you?"

Shit, they were wasting time. He needed to get to Hadley.

"Release her now," Ian said. "Or I'll have you arrested."

Bennett sensed a presence at his elbow. He glanced sideways, and spotted Killian in a tux.

Another man appeared. It was David Farrell.

Hadley's old boss flashed his badge. "SIS. I'm afraid we'll be taking your wife into custody, Mr. Wentworth."

The older man's face twisted as he realized this was real.

Kitty's face drained of color. "*No.* You can't do this."

"Shut up, Kitty," Ian snapped.

"It's not all fun and games now, is it?" Bennett swiveled to meet Killian's gaze. "Hadley?"

"Ajay got spooked and ran. She's chasing him in the street."

Kitty made a sound. They all swiveled to look at her.

"You know something," Bennett said.

"I have nothing to say." She lifted her pointy chin.

"We have recordings and evidence of what you've been doing, *Lady* Wentworth." Bennett let his gaze bore into her. "Talk. Now."

Some of her bravado leaked out.

"Kitty," her husband clipped. "If you know something—"

Her cheeks paled. "Nothing. Just that he wasn't supposed to leave. He was supposed to stay in the theatre."

"Why?" Bennett barked.

"That's all I know."

Unease coiled in Bennett. The exact same way he felt before a mission went to hell.

"Don't worry," Killian murmured. "Hadley isn't alone. I called in another of my team. Bram is following them."

Bennett nodded. "I'll find them. You've got this?"

Killian inclined his head.

Swiveling, Bennett headed for the exit, guests parting for him. He hit the front doors of the theater and lifted his phone to his ear.

"Hello, billionaire hottie," Hex's voice said.

"Hex, talk to me!"

"They're nearing the main square in Covent Garden. Bram's about a block behind. He's a big redhead. Can't miss him."

Bennett took off at a jog. He knew the maze of streets well. He pumped his arms and legs, moving into a sprint.

There were plenty of people around, but they darted out of his way. He raced out of a side street and into the main area of Covent Garden where the market buildings sat.

He spotted Hadley in one darkened corner and ran in that direction.

On the opposite side of the square, he saw a big form race out of another alley. It was the other Sentinel Security member, Bram "Excalibur" O'Donovan.

Hadley had Ajay cornered.

"Kitty's been arrested. Come with me now and we'll sort this out." Her voice was calm, like she was placating a wild animal.

Ajay swallowed. "No. I...I love Kitty. We haven't done anything wrong."

Bennett walked closer. Ajay saw him and jolted.

"Mr. Knightley. I'm...I'm really sorry. I didn't want to hurt you, or my friends at work, but Kitty said this was important. That Secura was supplying terrorists. She does favors for MI6 and I had to help her."

Bennett growled, but Hadley held up a hand. "Ajay, Kitty isn't MI6. She's working *with* the terrorists, and stealing from Secura."

The younger man shook his head wildly. "No. You have it wrong."

"What's in the bag, Ajay?" Hadley asked.

"I don't know. I was supposed to take it into the center of the theatre. Someone was going to meet me."

Bennett's heart thumped. *L'Orage.*

Ajay swallowed. "Look, can I talk to Kitty? We can clear this up."

"Kitty's been arrested by MI6," Bennett said. "She'll be interrogated."

"No. *No.*" Ajay frowned, reaching for the backpack strap. "This is getting hot."

"What?" Bennett said.

"It's burning." The younger man scrabbled to take the pack off.

Bennett's instincts screamed. He leaped at Hadley, tackling her to the ground.

Boom.

Heat washed over them. He heard Hadley cry out, felt objects pepper his back.

Old memories of other explosions pressed in on him. Bennett covered Hadley. He had to protect her. He had to keep her safe. He wouldn't let her be ripped apart.

Then pain exploded in his head and blackness engulfed him.

OH. *Fuck.*

Hadley's ears were ringing and Bennett's heavy weight crushed her into the rough, cobblestone street. Her palms stung from where they'd scraped on the ground, and she felt a burning sting on her left thigh.

Bomb.

Oh, hell. She turned her head and swallowed hard at the sight of smoking rubble.

She also saw something fleshy nearby and realized it was part of an arm.

Bile filled her mouth. *Poor, foolish Ajay.*

"Bennett?" She could hear shouts and screams in the distance, but everything was still a bit fuzzy.

That's when she realized Bennett was a dead weight; he wasn't moving.

"Bennett!" Her voice rose. Raw terror gripped her. A terror like she'd never felt before. "*Bennett*."

How badly was he hurt? Images raced through her—of his body torn up, of him bleeding to death.

She tried to move, but he was too heavy.

"Bennett, wake up and talk to me, dammit!"

She heard a groan, and she'd never heard a better sound. "Wake up, darling. You're squishing me."

"Hadley?" His voice sounded like gravel.

"That's right," she said.

"Hadley!" another deep male voice barked.

She saw Bram crouch down beside them.

"Help Bennett up," she said. "I'm fine."

Bennett's weight lifted off her and her lungs filled with oxygen. She sat up. Bennett was sitting beside her, his face dazed, one knee bent and the other out straight. His shirt was smeared with soot and dirt, and his hair was mussed. He had a scrape on his cheekbone, and a smear of blood at his temple.

The relief filling her made it hard to breathe. She cupped his cheek. His green-gold gaze met hers and she pressed her lips to his mouth, before moving her lips across his face and pressed a gentle kiss to his cheekbone.

"I'm very pleased you didn't get blown up," she said.

"Me too," he said.

She felt a lump at his temple. He must've bumped his head.

"You shielded me," she said.

"I've got plans for that body of yours, so I didn't want you getting hurt."

Nearby, Bram made an unhappy sound.

Hadley glanced at her friend. "Bram, Ajay's backpack was filled with explosives. Secure the scene."

Her friend looked relieved to have something to do. "Killian's on the way. Sure you're all right?"

She nodded.

He strode off, barking at the crowd to stay back.

Hadley turned her attention back to Bennett. "Any other injuries?"

He shook his head, then winced. "I'm fine. A little headache." But she watched as pain and anger suffused his face. "Ajay..."

"I'm sorry," she whispered.

"*Fuck.*"

She gripped his hands. "Kitty?"

"In custody."

"Good. We'll get the answers we need. We'll find whoever did this."

"He wanted this to go off in the theatre," Bennett said. "How many more will die before we catch him?"

"We'll get him, Bennett."

The wail of sirens announced the arrival of emergency services. The adrenaline was starting to fade, and pain had begun to creep in. Her hands and knees were scraped and bruised.

Bennett rose, and helped her up.

Damn, her legs were a little wobbly. She saw him

scan where the bomb had gone off, a grim look on his face.

David and Killian arrived. Her boss gave her a hard look. "You're both okay?"

She nodded, and he patted her arm.

"What a bloody mess," David said. "You sure you're both uninjured?"

Hadley nodded. "Just a few scrapes. You have Kitty Wentworth in custody. She knows who this L'Orage imposter is. Whoever they are, they're responsible for Ajay's death."

"Oh, we'll be asking Lady Wentworth plenty of questions," David said.

"I want to be there for the questioning," Bennett said.

"Not tonight." David looked at them both. "You look like you've been dragged through the gutter. I suggest you get out of here. The vultures—otherwise known as the press—will arrive soon like a pack of dogs. A bomb in Covent Garden is big enough news, but Bennett Knightley almost getting blown up will have them champing at the bit. Report in tomorrow. For now, get cleaned up and get some rest."

Bennett swallowed, looking frustrated. "Ajay's family —"

"We'll inform them. Go."

Killian gripped Hadley's shoulders, his sharp gaze on her face. "Do you need anything?"

She shook her head.

Bennett pulled out his phone and called Henry. She shivered, starting to feel cold now. They moved away from the main blast area, trying not to attract any attention.

A jacket settled over her shoulders, and she smiled at Bennett, but then her vision wavered.

He frowned. "Hadley? Are you okay?"

"Yes—"

Pain ripped through her thigh, turning to a sharp burn. Her knees buckled.

"Shit." He caught her, then lowered her to the ground. "What's wrong?"

"I...don't know. My thigh."

His hands ran up her leg, pushing her dress out of the way.

"There's a cut in your dress. *Dammit.* And it's wet. The black color hid the blood." He bared her leg. A one-inch piece of steel was embedded in her skin, and her thigh was covered in blood.

He hissed out a breath. "I'll get a medic—"

"No." She gripped his wrist. "Pull it out and put pressure on it. We need to get out of here."

A muscle worked in his jaw.

"Please, Bennett. You can clean this up. The last thing we need is for both of us to be splashed in the press. It will jeopardize the mission."

He was silent.

"Please?"

"Fine." He sounded like he was talking through clenched teeth. "If it gets worse, you're going to the hospital."

She nodded tiredly.

"Ready?" he asked.

"Yes."

He pulled the metal out. It hurt and she bit her tongue, but a small moan still escaped.

"Dammit to hell, Hadley."

She dragged in a deep breath. "It's okay. It's not that bad."

"Liar." He tore off the bottom of his shirt and wadded the fabric against her leg. "Hold that."

Then he scooped her up in his arms. She snuggled into the jacket and against the fierce warmth of him. He felt so good.

She rarely leaned on anyone, but she realized she was totally fine leaning on this man. Her cheeks heated, and she knew she was blushing.

Some time over the last few days, Bennett Knightley had earned her trust.

He carried her into a side alley, and she saw the Ferrari parked there, with Henry waiting for them beside it.

When he saw them approach, he cursed. He opened the passenger-side door. "She okay?"

"She will be." Bennett maneuvered into the passenger seat and settled Hadley in his lap.

"I can sit in the back." The sports car had two small seats in the back.

"No." He clipped the belt over both of them. "My place."

Henry nodded and started the engine.

Hadley snuggled into him. For now, she'd let him take care of things.

CHAPTER TWELVE

As Henry pulled into Bennett's building in Knightsbridge, Bennett was still struggling to get a handle on his violent fury.

His enemy had killed Ajay. Another of Bennett's people destroyed. Another person he'd failed to protect.

And the bastard had hurt Hadley.

He knew her wound was still bleeding, felt the wetness on his suit trousers.

This fucker would pay.

"You need any help?" Henry asked.

"I've got her." Bennett exited the car and hitched Hadley higher up in his arms. "Thanks, Henry."

"Call if you need anything."

"I can walk," Hadley said.

Bennett just shot her a look.

"Or not," she responded.

He had a private elevator to his penthouse and pressed his access card to the reader.

"I'm really sorry about Ajay, Bennett. Whatever his bad decisions, he didn't deserve this."

"No, he didn't." Bennett's thoughts turned to Hamed. "No one deserves to die like this."

The elevator stopped and he stepped inside his home. He carried her through to the living area.

"Wow, crappy place you have here," she said.

"Thanks."

He watched her taking it all in. He'd kept it to neutral tones—cream, wood, some touches of muted gray. He'd wanted it to feel comfortable, not like a show home. He carried her into his bedroom. The blinds were up, displaying the dark sweep of the park and the glitter of lights in the distance.

The lights beside his bed were on. The wall behind the bed had a gray textured surface and the bed head was a dark navy blue. A cream rug covered the wood floor and he strode across it into the bathroom.

"Oh, God, I could just live in your bathroom," she said.

He loved his bathroom, too. There was lots of white marble, with dark-gray accents, a huge shower, and a free-standing stone tub beside the floor to ceiling windows.

He had a clear image of her in here, in only her underwear, putting on her makeup, with him beside her putting on cufflinks.

Shit. He'd never, ever wanted a woman in his space, in his life, in any permanent way. Hadn't believed he deserved it.

Paul would never have that. Hamed and his wife would never have that.

But Hadley Lockwood was becoming a need he couldn't deny. Like the air he needed to breathe.

And if he told her, she'd run as fast as she could.

He set her on the small stool tucked into a space by the vanity. Then he pushed her dress up. The rag of his shirt was soaked through with blood.

"I'll get my first aid kit. Don't move."

"Yes, sir."

His lips quirked. "I see your sass is back, so you must be feeling okay."

Bennett hurried to his kitchen to grab his first aid kit. He came back, taking in those bare legs. So long and tempting.

Jesus, she's hurt, you bastard.

He got to work cleaning her cut. It was ragged, but not as deep as he'd feared. He smoothed a hand up her thigh, and she shivered.

"Painkillers." He fished some pills out of the box, then filled a glass with water, and handed them to her. She dutifully swallowed them.

"It doesn't hurt much," she said.

"I'm going to put a little glue on it, then bandage it."

"Yes, doctor."

"Be good, and you'll get a reward."

She arched a brow. "Really?"

"Really." He finished putting a bandage on the wound.

She pushed the skirt of her dress down. "Now you."

"What?"

"You were knocked unconscious, Bennett."

146

"For three seconds. I've had concussions before, and this is nothing."

"I don't care. Sit." She pointed at the edge of the tub.

He hesitated, but she shot him a look that said she wasn't letting him wriggle out of this. With a sigh, he sat.

She leaned in, gently probing the side of his head. He had a perfect view of her cleavage and groaned.

Hadley looked down and saw the direction of his gaze. "Really?"

"Hadley, I get hard when I see you from a distance, let alone if you put your beautiful breasts right in my face."

"I think you're fine. If your cock can still get hard, even though we were almost blown up, your head can't be that hurt."

He grunted.

She cleaned the scrapes on his head, then stepped back.

"I'm going to use your fancy shower now," she said.

Bennett cleared his throat. "I'll find you something to wear. If you need me, just call."

"I'll be fine."

He left her to it.

She was fine. She was fine. He kept repeating the words in his head as he snagged a shirt from his walk-in closet. He left it on his bed for her, then headed for one of his guest bathrooms.

He quickly showered, trying not to think of the bomb going off, of Ajay blown to pieces. *Poor Ajay.*

The images in Bennett's head morphed, and he saw Hamed injured and dying. The harsh rattle of his breath.

The fear in his friend's eyes as he'd understood he wasn't going to make it.

Why had Bennett survived, while Paul and Hamed hadn't?

Life is pain, man. Anyone who says differently is selling something. Paul had always said that during their missions. Quoting from some movie Bennett had forgotten.

You have the chance to live, my friend. Make the most of it. Cherish it. Hamed's voice, from one of their many long, after-mission conversations.

Bennett pressed his palms to the tiles, and let the water rain down over his head. He dragged in a breath.

In his head, he imagined Hadley hurt and bleeding. Dying.

No. She was alive, and naked in his shower.

They were both alive.

He turned off the shower, toweled dry, and dressed in long, black pajama pants. When he left the bathroom, Hadley was still in his en suite.

In the living area, he headed for the bar to pour himself a glass of Scotch. He reached for Balvenie 40-year-old. *What the hell?* He grabbed the Balvenie 60-year-old instead. He kept it for very special occasions. After pouring, he sank into his armchair.

He stared out the window and thought of Ajay. He sipped the Scotch, but tonight it tasted bitter.

He released a long breath.

There was a whisper of sound.

She appeared like an apparition, his white shirt looking ridiculously sexy on her.

Bennett didn't move.

Her fingers ran along his shoulders. "So tightly wound. You keep it all locked in, then you sit in the dark and brood."

"I'm not good company, Hadley."

"I don't mind." She sat in his lap, sliding an arm across his shoulders. She smelled like his citrus body wash. Fresh and good.

"I keep imagining that second when I realized there was a bomb," he said. "The moment it went off."

"And your first instinct was to protect me."

"You still got hurt."

"Barely." She took his glass and sipped, making a small murmur of appreciation. "This is good."

"It should be. It's over a hundred thousand pounds a bottle."

Her hand froze for a second, then she set the glass down on the side table. Her other hand fiddled with the damp hair at the base of his neck.

"Ajay is dead," he said. "Another young life cut short for no goddamn reason."

"You can't save everyone, Bennett." She leaned closer, her lips running along his jaw. It wasn't sexual exactly, more to comfort.

But he found everything about this woman sexual.

His hand gripped her hip.

"You know we can only try our best, and we can't be responsible for other people's choices. Ajay knew what he was doing." She met Bennett's gaze. "Hamed gave up his vest."

Bennett pressed his forehead to hers. "Doesn't make it easy to accept."

"I know." She peppered more kisses on his skin. "You're enough, Bennett, just as you are. You can't save everyone, you don't need to pay any penance."

He pressed his face against her lips, her words washing through him.

"I'm very glad we're alive, Mr. Knightley."

"Me too, Ms. Lockwood."

She nipped his jaw harder, and shifted her sweet arse, rubbing against his hardening cock.

"I think we should both celebrate that."

"MY CONTROL IS...SHAKY." Bennett's hands flexed on her. "I don't want to hurt you."

"You won't." This man was a protector. Hadley nibbled at his lips. "And I don't mind it a little rough."

He groaned. His cock was like a steel rod under her ass.

She couldn't fight the riotous emotion she felt for this man anymore. She was very glad they were both alive and relatively unhurt.

It could've been a very different story.

She fastened her mouth on his. His strong arms tightened around her, and the kiss turned rich and potent, overwhelming.

A wild, reckless energy filled her. She *needed* him. Needed him so badly.

He cupped one of her breasts and she moaned. She needed her hands on him.

She stroked his shoulders, down his bare chest. He was all hard muscles, with a smattering of brown hair. She felt several old scars under her fingertips. Proof of the warrior he was.

He squeezed her breast again, and need twisted inside her. She *craved* him.

"I want to put my mouth on these." He flicked open a button of the shirt.

She shifted off his lap and stood.

"Lights on low," he said.

Low lights flickered on, giving the room a dull, golden glow. He was sprawled in the chair like a big lion, alert and ready to go in for the kill. Or an emperor, waiting for his concubine.

She glanced at the windows. "People could see."

"The windows are treated with a special film. I like my privacy."

Still, it gave her a little thrill to imagine that someone could watch them.

She unbuttoned the shirt and slipped it off.

She saw Bennett's hands clenched on the armrests of his chair.

"Fuck me," he breathed. "I've been imagining what you had on under your dress all night."

Luckily, she hadn't gotten any blood on the bodysuit made of mostly sheer fabric that showed off more than it concealed. The deep V plunged to her belly button.

He spread his legs. "Come here."

She stepped forward and she saw the moment his gaze dropped to where her pussy was on display for him.

"*Fuck.*" His voice was low, vibrating with desire.

He slid a hand between her legs and stroked her already slick folds over the barely-there lace.

"You like this?" she asked.

His hot gaze flicked up to hers. "Did you wear it for me?"

"No, I wore it for me. It was just a bonus if you liked it, too."

He growled. "Turn around."

She turned slowly. The bodysuit had even less at the back. A black ribbon that tied at her lower back, and a thong-style bottom.

He groaned again, his hands cupping her hips and pulling her closer toward him.

He spun her and tumbled her onto his lap.

"It's sexy as hell, but it's you I want." He pulled the ribbon loose at the back, then nudged the lace off her shoulders, displaying her breasts. Then he roughly yanked the bodysuit down her body. She moved her legs, helping, and he tossed the lingerie away.

It was extra sexy to be lying there naked in his arms. He lowered his head, his mouth moving across her breasts.

"Oh, yes." She pushed against the wet heat of his mouth, a cry breaking free. Desire shifted into even higher gear.

As he cupped both her breasts, kneading and pushing them together, he sucked on a nipple, Hadley moaned.

He shifted to the other breast, taking his time. She slid her hands into his hair.

She was slick between her thighs, no doubt leaving a mark on his trousers.

The sensations were too much, but not enough. She'd never needed like this before.

"*Bennett.*"

"It's all right. I've got you, Hadley. You're safe."

That deep voice was like a drug.

The need for sweet release was clawing at her. She reached between their bodies and palmed his cock.

"No." He caught her wrist. "I want you to come first."

"I want you inside me." Her voice was husky.

"You want to rush. You want to take the hit without the intimacy."

She felt a stab of fear. "Bennett, I want you to fuck me."

"I will. Soon." He nipped her breast again. "I think we'll head to the bedroom, though."

He rose with her in his arms. He carted her around so easily, and his strength was intoxicating.

In the shadowed bedroom, he laid her on the big bed.

When he shoved his loose trousers off, she saw how hard that cock was. Her belly clenched. It was thick, and hard, rising up toward his abs.

"I want you," she murmured.

"I know, beautiful." He pressed a knee to the bed. Then he ran a hand down her body, from shoulder to thigh. The look in his eyes made her shiver.

When he touched the bandage on her leg, he moved over her, and pressed a gentle kiss to it.

God. Her belly was alive with sensations, not all ones she liked.

He was making her feel dangerous things.

Then he moved over her, his mouth on hers. He kissed her, pouring everything into it.

She kissed him back. Lost in it. In him. She arched into him.

Then he went lower, his mouth closing over one nipple again. One of his hands slid between her thighs, stroked, then two fingers pushed inside her.

Electricity raced through Hadley's body.

Too much. The hard pull of his mouth, the press of his fingers.

She felt taken over. Owned. Swept away.

"*Bennett.*" Her voice was a little shaky.

He must've heard it. "I've got you, beautiful. I'll take care of you, I promise. Now let go. Scream for me."

His mouth dragged over her quivering belly, then it was between her legs. His lips closed over her clit and sucked.

"Now, Hadley."

She had no choice but to tip over into hot pleasure.

She screamed, her vision sparking with spots of light and every muscle in her body contracting, then releasing. Pleasure was a violent rush.

Oh. *God.*

She lay there panting, her skin sensitized, her belly filled with heat. When she could finally see and think again, he was beside her, a faint smile on his face. But there was too much dark need on his features for him to look relaxed or happy.

Throat thick, she swallowed.

She needed more of him. And she needed to see him as out of control as her.

Hadley pounced.

She straddled him, shoving him flat on his back.

Her hands closed on his thick cock.

This was what she needed. This big warrior spread out for her. She'd take him, and make him want her as much as she wanted him.

CHAPTER THIRTEEN

H e felt desire pumping off her.

Bennett stared at her beautiful face. Hadley's desire was underscored with a little touch of desperation. No, not desperation. Fear.

"Slow down," he said, catching her hips before she drove herself down on his cock.

"I want you inside me. *Now.*"

Bennett rolled, pinning her beneath him. "We're not going to rush this." He reached for the bedside table and opened the drawer. He pulled out a strip of condoms and threw them on the bed.

"I want you to feel everything," he said. "Enjoy everything."

Her gaze was a little wild, her chest heaving.

"I'm going to make it good for you," he told her.

"Knightley—"

"Bennett. Here, I'm Bennett."

He felt her tremble.

He rose up to his knees, his cock rising up high and

thick. It took him seconds to rip open the condom and roll it on. Hadley watched every move.

Then he lowered his body to hers, pushing her thighs apart. He notched the head of his cock at her pussy, and slowly pushed himself inside her.

Her lips parted and she moaned. "I can feel every inch of you." She gripped his arms, her nails biting in.

Bennett savored the look on her face, watching her feel every bit of him. It cost him to keep a savage grip on his control.

Then he thrust deep, all the way to the hilt, and she cried out.

"You and me, Hadley," he gritted out. "This is right where I'm supposed to be."

He drew back, and plunged inside her again. He couldn't stop thrusting faster, harder.

The pleasure was growing, fierce and hot.

There was shock in her eyes, her husky cries filling the room. Her eyes glazed over as she gripped him tight.

"*Bennett.*"

"Come, Hadley. Your pleasure first. Let me watch you."

She arched, crying out.

Clenching his jaw, Bennett held back his own release. He wanted to watch her come again. He rolled them so she was above him. He yanked her down, his cock thrusting deep.

"Again," he ordered.

Her back bowed, her hips moving in a fluid dance. He felt brutal pleasure clamping down on the base of his spine.

He wouldn't last long.

He reached out and found her swollen clit, rubbed.

A guttural cry came from her.

"Come again, Hadley. Give it to me."

Throwing her head back, she screamed his name.

Her climax was like claws ripping at him. His hands gripped her hips and with a growl, he flipped her, shoving her onto her back.

He pulled her hips up and thrust inside her. He pistoned into her hot body. Her nails scraped, sharp and quick, on his back.

"Come for me now," she whispered in his ear.

With one last, wild thrust, he emptied himself inside her, groaning her name.

In that blinding moment, he knew he'd do anything for this woman. Give her everything she needed. Keep her safe until his last breath.

HADLEY LAY SPRAWLED on Bennett's chest. They were both slick with sweat.

As she came down from the high, and yes, it was a stratospheric one, anxiety crept in like smoke. He'd broken her open. She had no defenses left.

"I should go," she whispered.

She tried to move, but a big hand on her back kept her pinned in place.

She growled. "Knightley, I'm going."

"No."

She felt a spurt of anger. "You don't get a say. You got your orgasm—"

"And you got three. You owe me."

She sucked in a sharp breath. "You arrogant—"

He rolled, and started to pull his cock free of her body.

Damn. She bit her lip. He felt huge despite them both just coming.

Then he caught her gaze, and thrust back inside her.

The move set off a bunch of pleasurable aftershocks and she gasped.

"You're not going," he said. "I want you again, and you want me inside you again."

She licked her lips.

Bennett cupped her cheek. "You're not alone, Hadley."

She looked into his eyes, and saw the raw need that echoed the feeling in her belly.

"Now, stay here," he ordered. "I'll be right back. And if you aren't right there, I will hunt you down."

She nodded.

She watched him rise from the bed and head for the bathroom. His ass was pure, masculine perfection. Hard, muscular, biteable. There was an ugly scar on his lower back, and she bit her lip. It looked like a shrapnel wound.

She heard the toilet flush and water run. Then she got a front view as he walked back to the bed. His cock was hard again.

"Well, if Secura doesn't work out, you could do nude modeling," she said.

He grunted, then reached for something on the bedside table. "I have a gift for you."

She groaned. "Another one?"

He smiled and handed her the flat box.

Hadley opened it and saw a pair of tiny, red-lace panties. She arched a brow.

"I stole your other pair in my office the other night. I figured I owed you."

"And there is no benefit for you."

His smile widened. "Don't bother putting them on." He grabbed another condom and opened it. She watched him roll it on.

Then he loomed over her. "Now, let's see if I can change your mind about doggy style."

"Oh." Hadley decided to stop worrying and just let herself feel. "Okay."

Several hours later, Hadley couldn't fault Bennett's effort and enthusiasm. She was exhausted by everything they'd done to each other. His big body was now curled protectively around hers, and she felt warm and safe.

He pressed a kiss to the top of her head.

She tipped her head back and he nuzzled her neck, one of his hands sliding down her body to cup her ass.

This felt...nice. Intimate and safe. Unease tried to push in.

"Hadley, stop thinking. Go to sleep."

She forced herself to relax. "Stop being bossy."

He squeezed her ass cheek. "Sleep, or I'll fuck you again."

"That doesn't make me want to sleep, Knightley."

"But you need some rest. Sleep now, and I promise to fuck you in the morning."

SHE SNUCK out of the bed.

It was still early, and the room was awash in silver light.

Hadley looked back. Bennett looked delicious.

He was sprawled on his side, one arm tucked under her pillow. That big male body was strong, and she suddenly realized he had a small tattoo on his side. She wanted to explore it.

But a part of her was a panicked mess and needed some space.

She found a silky, black robe in his closet. It didn't look like it had been worn, and she couldn't picture Bennett in it. She slipped it on and headed into the living room.

His place was stunning and she loved it.

His interior designer had earned their money. She cocked her head. She'd add a few more plants and maybe some more eye-catching artwork. Something dark and moody.

She wasn't running. She stroked her hand over the back of the couch, enjoying the feel of the suede. She licked her lips. She just needed to get her head straight. She wasn't used to feeling uncertain and unsure of herself.

She didn't like it. Since Casper, she'd made her life

exactly what she wanted. She took risks professionally, but not personally.

A part of her didn't want these feelings for Bennett.

Another part of her whispered that it was already too late.

She spotted her discarded bodysuit and took a second to slip it on, smiling at Bennett's reaction to it. She pulled the robe back on and headed for the kitchen. She was a decent cook, so she decided to make breakfast.

God, his kitchen was something else. The best, high-end appliances, enormous stove, and glossy stone countertops.

Soon she had the coffee machine running and was cooking up an omelet.

"Good morning."

The sleep-gruff voice made her turn.

Bennett stood there, shirtless, with only his loose, black sleep trousers on. The waistband sat low, showing off lean hip bones and the tantalizing muscles and abs.

"Morning," she said.

"My brother bought me that robe for Christmas one year as a joke. Said all playboy billionaires should have a black, silk robe." He strolled closer. "I've never worn it. I was going to donate it."

Then he reached for her, and pushed the fabric off one of her shoulders, and kissed her skin. She shivered.

"Glad I kept it. It looks good on you, Hadley." He paused. "When I woke up alone, I expected you to be gone."

"I'm not a total coward."

"You're the least cowardly person I know."

She reached over and turned off the burner. "The omelet is ready."

He toyed with the bit of sheer lace he'd uncovered at her shoulder. "I'm suddenly not hungry for eggs."

Tingles started up all over. How the hell could she want him like this again so soon?

Just enjoy, Hadley. Stop dissecting everything.

She backed away from him, and slipped the robe off. It pooled at her ankles.

His gaze traced the lingerie.

"That thing is designed to tempt a man to make bad decisions." He walked toward her.

She stepped onto the rug in the living room, her toes sinking into the plush pile. The heat in his gaze scorched her, and she was amazed she didn't catch fire.

"Turn around." His voice lowered.

She turned.

Then he was on her.

He pushed her toward the leather couch, fingers digging into her hips. His hands stroked between her legs.

She knelt on the leather cushions and gripped the back of the couch.

"It's going to be hard, Hadley. Hard and fast."

She looked back at him. "Good."

He shoved his trousers off. His cock was hard and swollen. She heard the crinkle of a wrapper.

Anticipation twisted inside her belly.

"You're the sexiest damn woman I've ever seen." His hand shaped over her hips. He tugged at the lace between her legs, toying with it, nudging it aside.

Then he covered her, and his thick cock slammed inside her, impaled her.

"Bennett!"

He stilled, hands moving around her shoulders. "Did I hurt you?"

"No. God, no. Move, Bennett."

He moved.

She rocked back to meet his heavy thrusts.

"Christ, you're tight. You like it hard, don't you, beautiful?" He covered her, his chest hot against her back. He bit her ear and she moaned. "You're so elegant, cultured, but under it you're strength and steel. You can take it hard."

Hadley couldn't think or process anything. She was lost in the intense pleasure. Lost in him. Her fingers dug into the couch.

"Touch yourself," he groaned. "I want us to come together."

She slid a hand under her body. She felt where Bennett's cock drove into her. Her muscles clenched and he groaned. Then she found her clit.

But just as the pleasure was growing, his thrusts slowed. They were still firm, solid, and deliberate, and she could feel every slide.

"Feel that, Hadley?" he murmured.

"Bennett..."

"You and me. Feel how I fit here, just right. Like I belong."

An intense mix of emotions hit her.

"*Mine.*" He thrust faster again, his hand sliding around her hip to cover hers. They rubbed her clit together. "I know what you need. Everything you need."

Hadley's orgasm ripped through her, his name torn from her lips. She clawed at the couch, searching for an anchor.

With another hard thrust, Bennett came, his groan long and tortured.

Then she just stared at the dark leather, listening to their labored breathing. Pleasure still shuddered through her like little electric shocks.

He pulled out, then pressed his lips to her spine. She shivered.

He helped her up, and his kiss to her lips was a sweet one. Then he retrieved the robe and wrapped her in it, before quickly dealing with the condom.

Hadley didn't move, she was still processing and trying to get her brain working.

"Hadley?"

She swallowed. "You said a lot of things."

"I could say it was the heat of the moment, but I meant them all."

She sucked in a breath.

He cupped her jaw. "You're mine, even if you can't admit it yet."

"Bennett." She pushed her hair back. "I have no idea how to belong to someone. I don't know how to give you what you deserve."

He stroked her skin. "I know it's scary. I'm not even sure I deserve you."

She made an angry sound.

"But I do know that to get something that's worth it,

you have to take a risk, and you have to believe," he said. "All I know is that I want you."

A cell phone rang.

"That's mine," he said.

She watched him answer it, emotions warring inside her.

"Okay, we'll be there shortly." He slipped the phone away, his face hard. "They're ready to question Kitty Wentworth."

Hadley straightened. "Good. We need to stop by my place first so I can get some clothes."

CHAPTER FOURTEEN

W ith his arms crossed over his chest, Bennett stared through the two-way glass.

The MI6 interrogator was good. The woman was calm but relentless. She looked to be his mother's age, with short, silver hair and an ageless face. And a ruthless skill at questioning.

Kitty Wentworth meanwhile was a crying mess at the table. She'd started out with cocky bluster, but it had slowly given way to panic and despair. Especially upon hearing that her husband was already organizing divorce papers.

"Who is your contact?" Helene, the interrogator, asked.

"I don't know him. I've *never* seen him."

"Yet you blindly followed his instructions? Without knowing who he was? You slept with men that he told you to sleep with?"

Kitty swallowed, all the elegance gone. She looked a decade older, her face lined and her hair tangled.

"It was just...fun. He gave me purpose. I agreed with his cause. We send our soldiers off to these god-awful places to die. I wanted to help, and it was more than just pilates, lunches, and shopping. It was nice to be wanted, needed."

"How did he contact you?"

Kitty sighed. "Online. I was bored. Discontent."

Beside Bennett, Hadley made an annoyed sound. "Yes, she had money to do whatever she liked, and she was bored. She could have found a hundred charities that needed her money and time."

He knew she was thinking about Nightingale House.

"I was trapped by society," Kitty continued. "I was expected to do certain things, act a certain way. I married so young."

"God, she makes me sick," Hadley said. "It's everyone else's fault."

"It's easier to justify her own poor choices that way," Killian said. The head of Sentinel Security was standing on the other side of Hadley.

"I joined some online groups. They were about the law of attraction, and manifesting what you want in your life. Westley contacted me there."

"Westley?" Helene prompted.

"He just uses the one name."

Bennett listened as Kitty talked about how she'd first met Westley. "Fuck."

"Westley groomed her, too," Killian said. "He found an unhappy, unfulfilled woman to do what he needed. Made her feel special, made her feel like she was doing something important."

"It doesn't make her any less responsible," Hadley said.

"She helped kill Ajay. She messed up Archie's life." Bennett kept a stranglehold on his emotions. "I want her to pay."

"She will." Hadley took his hand. "Her life has just imploded. She's going to jail."

The door opened, and David appeared. "Morning." He eyed Hadley and Bennett, his gaze lingering on their joined hands. "You're both doing okay today?"

"We're fine," Hadley said.

"Yes, we rested after last night's events." Bennett met her gaze, and he could tell she was thinking of all the ways they *hadn't* rested.

Hell. Hadley Lockwood fried his brain.

"Good," David said. "We'll keep working on Kitty. We need to know if there are more moles at Secura. And she must know something that can help us track down this damn Westley."

Bennett's phone vibrated. He pulled it out and saw lots of messages from Maudie. He thumbed through them.

"Everything okay?" Hadley asked.

"Maudie's sent a bunch of messages. Says there's something urgent at work."

"There's nothing more you can do here," David said. "Helene will keep up the interrogation."

Killian nodded. "Hadley, for now, keep your cover. Make sure there are no more leaks at Secura." The man frowned. "I feel like this isn't over."

Hadley and Bennett made their way to his car. He'd

taken his Bentley Continental GT today. The sleek, silver sports car was his second favorite in his collection.

"It's not good if Killian has a bad feeling," Hadley said. "His bad feelings are legendary for being right."

Bennett grunted. They got in the car and left MI6, heading for the Secura office.

"Who the hell is this Westley?" Bennett said.

"Someone who wants to hurt you." She turned to face him. "You must know who it is. This feels very personal."

"Maybe someone from Afghanistan uncovered my identity? It's not exactly a secret that I was SAS."

She frowned, nibbling her lip. It brought back memories of the night before.

Damn. The last thing he needed right now was an erection.

"Well, keep thinking," she said. "Maybe something will pop." She eyed him. "Bennett?"

"Hmm?"

"You're thinking about sex."

"Beautiful, I do that anytime I'm around you. And now that I know how it feels to sink inside you, it's just made it worse."

There was a faint touch of pink on her cheeks. "Bennett."

"Don't tell me you aren't thinking about it, too."

"We have work to do."

"I can multitask." He touched her thigh. "I'm going to be thinking about when I can touch you again next."

He saw the glimmer of uncertainty on her face before she hid it.

"Stop freaking me out," she said.

He squeezed her leg. "I know it's scary, but I'm not going anywhere. I'm not going to betray you. I'm doing the opposite. I'm here for you. Always."

"Freaking me out."

He squeezed her leg again.

They reached Secura, and he drove into the parking garage. As they exited the car, a big form strode in their direction.

Bram.

"You all right?" the big man asked.

"Fine, Bram." Hadley hugged her friend.

Watching them, Bennett felt a twist in his gut. She clearly trusted this man, and Killian. As the big redhead wrapped his strong arms around Hadley, Bennett didn't like it.

Jeez, he needed to get his inner possessive prick under control.

Hadley stepped back. "They're interrogating Kitty Wentworth. Nothing useful yet."

"Killian updated me," Bram said. "He said I'm supposed to hang around here. Back you up if you need it. The boss didn't like you almost getting blown up."

"I didn't like it either," she said with a frown. "Why did L'Orage—I mean, Westley—do that? Give Kitty a bag of explosives to give to Ajay?"

Bennett shrugged. "Kitty said she didn't know it contained explosives."

"Westley knew," Hadley murmured. "And Ajay was supposed to head straight into the heart of the theatre and detonate it." She lifted her head. "Right where you'd be."

Bennett frowned. "You think he was trying to kill me?"

"I think everything has been about hurting you in some way. I think Archie was the opening shot to get your attention, and Ajay was upping the ante. Westley knew you were onto Kitty. The explosives were for you, Bennett. He tried to kill you."

Bennett shook his head. "If he was trying to kill me, it was a dumb plan. Too many things could go wrong. Did go wrong."

"It doesn't matter. Even if it didn't kill you, he knew it would rattle you, and kill one of your employees."

Bennett frowned.

"Any words on the type of explosives?" Bram asked. "You can tell a lot from how they're made."

Hadley shook her head. "All we know is that they were military grade. They're still being examined."

The three of them headed into the Secura office.

"Bram, if anyone asks, you're a communications consultant and we have a meeting," she said.

The big man scowled. "Communications consultant?"

Bennett hid a grin. Bram was the least likely person to be a communications consultant. He looked like an old-fashioned warrior in a suit; he just needed some warpaint streaked on his face and a broadsword in his hand.

Bennett was trying to figure out a way to steal a kiss from Hadley when Maudie raced over. His assistant was practically jogging, an uncharacteristic look of panic on her face. Her blonde curls were extra wild today.

He frowned. "Maudie—?"

"You should answer your messages," she snapped at him.

"What's wrong?"

She blew out a breath, ruffling her hair. "The phones are ringing off the hook. Reporters. Word is out that Secura is selling goods to terrorist organizations."

Bennett's stomach dropped. *Fuck.* He glanced at Hadley.

"Go," she said. "Deal with it, and I'll touch base with the communications team."

Grinding his teeth together, Bennett headed straight to his office.

———

A THROBBING HEADACHE had taken up residence behind her right eye.

Hadley sighed and rested an elbow on her desk. She'd kept up her Secura cover job, working round-the-clock with the communications team to try and fight the fires of all the media stories taking over the press. She'd also done some work with Hex, trying to find out who Westley was.

Someone was out to get Bennett, and she was going to find out who.

And stop them.

He might leave her confused, and feeling things she didn't want to feel, but she wouldn't let anyone hurt him.

"I *will* find you."

Hex was turning over Bennett's life, looking for who

might be responsible. It was looking more and more likely this was due to his time in the military. All his missions were classified.

She touched her laptop. A photo of Hamed appeared. There was another one of the interpreter with Bennett, grinning. Their friendship and respect for each other was obvious.

There was another shot of the pair with Bennett's SAS team. Some of the faces were blurred—they were still active military. A few were not. She saw one young, blond man, his arm slung around a grizzled, dark-haired veteran. Their faces weren't blurred out because they were dead.

She glanced out her office door. Bennett's door was still closed. He'd been so busy today. She'd only glimpsed him once, and his face had looked carved from rock, but she could tell there was contained fury under the surface.

The stories running in the media were not good, to put it mildly. Someone had leaked that Secura gear was being sold to terrorists. That shipments meant for aid groups and foreign military hadn't arrived, or had been delayed.

The media was spinning it as a money grab. A greedy billionaire out for more money.

A few reputable places were reporting about the lost and stolen shipments. But the rest of the gutter trash was coming up with the wildest, most salacious headlines. They were quoting "sources close to Bennett," saying that he was a money-hungry playboy more interested in fast cars and ski trips. One paper had dredged up a picture of him in the Alps, grinning while skiing. It looked to be several years old, but no one would care.

Her throat tightened. She wanted to scream at these people for judging him, telling lies.

He'd started Secura in the hopes of helping, so she knew all this garbage would cut him deeply.

Hadley paused. It would hurt him. Was designed to hurt him.

It wasn't a coincidence. The mysterious Westley was behind this. He'd leaked the story to the press.

Whoever Westley was, he didn't want Bennett digging into him. That meant Kitty knew something, and Westley didn't want them to find it.

That was if Westley knew Kitty was in custody. People had seen her arrest, but MI6 had managed to keep it out of the press.

Hadley grabbed her phone and sent a message to David. She mentioned that maybe Westley didn't know Kitty was in custody.

> We've left her phone on and have access to her computer. She's willing to do anything to cut a deal.

Hadley snorted. No doubt.

> She is the key, David.

> We'll get whoever Westley is. How's Knightley holding up?

She heard shouting from Bennett's office.

> Not great. You've seen the reports in the press?

Yes.

> I'm pretty sure Westley is behind it.

We're closing in.

Hadley checked a few more messages and emails. Bram had left a few hours ago to join Killian.

Soon, the Secura office was almost empty. Maudie appeared in the doorway, looking tense and tired.

"Halle... Can you check on him?"

The woman's tone was worried. Hadley had only ever heard Maudie snarky.

"He's had a rough day," Maudie said.

"You're worried about him."

The young woman looked self-conscious. "I'm his assistant, so it's my job to worry." She paused. "You'll ensure he leaves soon?"

"I will. Good night, Maudie."

"He's in conference room two. Everyone else is gone."

Hadley nodded and shut down her laptop. Then she went in search of Bennett.

There was silence in the office, and lights were either off, or dimmed. She paused at the conference room door.

Bennett sat in a chair at the head of the table. He looked rumpled, and he'd clearly run his hands through his hair numerous times. He was staring at the floor.

She hated seeing him so tired and stressed.

"Hey."

His head lifted. "Ms. Atwood."

"There's no one left in the office."

"Ms. Lockwood, then."

"Rough day?"

He gave an unhappy laugh. "You could say that."

"This will pass," she said. "The communications team has been working overtime fighting fires today."

"No one cares about the truth, Hadley. Especially when the lies are much more interesting, and stir up anger and outrage."

She walked over to him and stood in front of him, pressing her hands to his shoulders. "It will pass."

"But it'll leave a stain."

"This is Westley taking more shots at you. You do good work, Bennett. Don't forget that."

He nodded. "It's just been a shitty day."

She ran a hand over his stubble covered jaw. "Why don't I see if I can make it a little better?"

She felt a spark of shock at just how much she wanted to comfort him. To help him carry this weight.

His hands lifted to her hips. "Hadley—"

"It's okay, Bennett. Just stop thinking for a bit." She tipped his head back and kissed him.

His mouth moved under hers, then suddenly he surged up and lifted her off her feet. He set her on the conference table.

She pressed into him, the kiss hot and wild. A moan vibrated through her, and she slid her hands into his hair.

"I feel like the pressure's been building all day," he growled.

"I'm here," she panted.

The next kiss was harder.

"Now," he bit out.

She gripped his shirt and ripped downward. Buttons pinged on the glossy table.

He tugged at her skirt, shoving it up to her hips. Then he pushed her back to lie on the table, with a hard yank, her panties were gone.

"I don't have a condom," he said.

"I'm clean and protected." She met his hot gaze.

"My last checkup was clean, and I've always used condoms," he said.

She swallowed. "I trust you, Bennett." She pressed her palms to his chest, raked her nails down his abs, then snagged her fingers on his trousers.

"Fuck. I can take you bare." His tone was shaky, almost touched with awe.

He pushed her hands away with jerky movements, then ripped his trousers open. Then he yanked her legs around his hips, and quickly stroked her pussy.

She was wet already and cried out. "*Hurry.*"

"I missed you all day." He bent over her, then thrust hard inside her.

It wrenched a cry from her. She raised her arms above her head.

The look on his face was fierce, and her belly clenched. He liked seeing her spread out for him.

He pulled back and thrust again. He stretched her to her limits. Filled her.

"Move, Bennett. Take what you need."

His hips pistoned as he thrust inside her.

Their grunts and moans filled the room, and time seemed to blur. All she could do was feel.

Hadley tightened her legs around him, holding on as he pounded into her. It was lucky the conference table was huge, or it would be moving with each thrust.

"I'm going to come, beautiful," he growled.

"Do it." She was so close.

He kept up his relentless assault. It felt so damn good.

Her climax hit like a tsunami. She cried out, her legs convulsing on him.

Bennett thrust deep, bent over her, and gripped her face. His mouth took hers in a fierce kiss. She watched him as his own release shook through him.

"Fucking Christ," he groaned. Then he slumped over her. "Hell, Hadley."

She lazily stroked his back. "I know this is a bespoke shirt. I should feel bad about ruining it."

He laughed. He sounded far less tense. "I don't give a shit about the shirt." He let out a long sigh. "You made a shitty day much better. Thank you."

"Oh, it was a hardship."

He hugged her. She hugged him back, vowing for the first time in her life to protect a man. A man she was starting to think of as hers.

CHAPTER FIFTEEN

B ennett woke, and for the first time in his life, wished he could just stay in bed for the entire day.

Hadley was sprawled over him, wearing a tiny excuse for a nightgown. Her brown hair spilled everywhere. He'd learned that she sprawled and didn't curl up. It was clear she wasn't used to sharing a bed, which he was damn happy about.

He ran a hand down her back, and she made a contented noise.

She'd share his bed. Hopefully for the rest of their lives.

"I'm keeping you," he whispered.

Luckily, she wasn't awake to hear and run off. After they caught Westley, and Secura was safe, Bennett would plan how to convince Hadley Lockwood to take a chance on him. On them.

He slid out of the bed, amused when she snuggled into his pillow and claimed more of the mattress.

He pulled on his workout gear and went to his home

gym. He'd worked up a sweat by the time she appeared, wearing his black robe and her hair still mussed from sleep.

"Hmm, there is nothing quite like a sweaty man with his muscles on display," she said.

Bennett flexed his biceps.

She grinned at him and wandered in. "It would be even better if you were shirtless."

Instantly, he ripped his T-shirt over his head.

She gave his chest and abs an appreciative look, then her face turned serious. "How are you today?"

"I'm okay." He grabbed a towel and wiped his face. "There are more factual articles being reported this morning. And a politician was caught having sex in his car...with a woman who wasn't his wife."

"Ah, how thoughtful of him."

"Yes, especially since she's his teenaged daughter's best friend. So, it's already dominating the headlines." His lips quirked. "Plus, hot, wild conference-table sex is pretty cathartic."

She smiled. "So it is."

He moved over to her and kissed her. "Thanks for taking care of me."

After hot sex on the conference room table, they'd come back to his place and she'd cooked dinner for him, and they'd opened a bottle of wine.

He hadn't realized that a quiet night with the right woman could be so damn perfect.

She cupped his cheek. "You're welcome."

She didn't look uneasy as she said that. His heart tightened. *Progress.*

"Now, go and shower," she said. "I'll make us an omelet that hopefully we'll eat hot today."

He snaked an arm around her. "How about you join me in the shower? It would be good for the environment, and I need someone to wash my back."

"Not a bad business case, Mr. Knightley."

He tightened his hold and lifted her. He tossed her over his shoulder, enjoying her squeal of laughter.

AFTER A RATHER LONG SHOWER, that while extremely pleasurable, probably wasn't that great for the environment, Bennett sat at the kitchen island while Hadley cooked.

He kept getting sidetracked. She wore wide-legged, black slacks, and a one-shouldered twist of dark-green fabric that formed a very interesting shirt. His gaze kept straying to her bare shoulder.

He made himself check his messages and emails. She swiveled and expertly served up the omelets.

"This smells great," he said.

"I'm a woman of many talents."

He ate a forkful and moaned. "Tastes great too."

They were only half finished when her phone rang. He saw some of the easy happiness bleed out of her eyes.

"It's Killian." She put the phone on speaker. "Hey, Kill."

"Hadley. Knightley. I'm at MI6. Wentworth cooperated, and Westley made contact."

Bennett sucked in a breath.

"You and Knightley get down here. Now."

"We're on our way." She met Bennett's gaze.

He nodded and rose. "Let's go. I guess half an omelet isn't bad."

Her lips quirked. "We'll get to eat a full breakfast together one day."

They wasted no time getting to MI6. Once they passed through security, they headed up to where Kitty was being held.

David and Killian met them there.

"What have you got?" Bennett asked.

"Westley emailed," David said. "We tried to track it, but our guys couldn't follow the trail. It was bounced through several servers in several different countries."

"Hex got a little bit further," Killian said. "The call originated in Romania, but she couldn't narrow it down any more than that."

"So the fucker isn't very far away," Bennett said.

"And he's on his way here," Killian said.

Hadley sucked in a breath, and Bennett stiffened.

"He asked Kitty if she was compromised," David said. "She did an impressive job of telling him that Bennett was breathing down her neck, but she'd managed to avoid him so far. Westley wants to meet her in person."

Bennett felt a leap of excitement. "When? Where?"

"Tomorrow," Killian said.

"At the wedding of Kitty's son," David finished.

"Hell," Bennett said.

"There will be a big crowd, and it's being held at a private country estate," Killian said. "Easy for him to stay hidden."

Hadley crossed her arms. "I don't like this. He could know we're onto him. This could be a trap."

"It's a risk we have to take," Bennett said.

Whatever it took, Westley was going down.

Hadley watched Bennett steadily, something steely flaring in her eyes. She nodded.

"We're going to release Kitty—" David began.

"What?" Bennett barked.

"She needs to do her normal routine and be at the wedding. She'll be monitored."

Bennett cursed and ran a hand through his hair.

"So, we'll all be at the wedding," Hadley said.

"Yes, undercover," David said. "Killian and Hadley, you're going in as guests, along with your man Bram. Knightley, you're too recognizable."

"I'm going," Bennett bit out. There was no way in hell he'd not be there.

David's mouth flattened. "Listen—"

"Bennett can go undercover with the catering team," Hadley said. "No one will be looking for a billionaire serving food and drinks."

Bennett shot her a grateful look.

The MI6 boss' face twisted but he finally nodded. "Fine. I'll have agents seeded throughout the guests. It's a country estate with a stately home, just outside of London. I'm sending in a tech team today to put up cameras. It will be fully monitored."

"I guess I need another dress," Hadley said.

Bennett couldn't help but smile. Of course, she had to go shopping. "So, by tomorrow afternoon we could have this bastard."

"We *will* have him," Hadley said.

"All right, go," David said. "Keep up your regular work routine. Don't arouse any suspicions."

Bennett pulled in a breath. Tomorrow this could all be over.

"Come on, boss." Hadley elbowed him.

"Hmm, I like you calling me that."

She rolled her eyes.

HADLEY REALLY, really liked Bennett's Bentley Continental GT. It was sleek classy, but not too flashy like the Ferrari.

They were headed to the Secura office, and she was eager to plan out the operation for the wedding tomorrow.

Finally, they could catch this Westley. Her belly tightened. She didn't want Bennett hurt.

She glanced at him in the driver's seat, gaze tracing the strong line of his jaw. She knew how far he'd go to protect his company and people.

Just a week ago, she'd thought him just another rich, pushy man with his own agenda.

Now, everything had changed.

"We need to prep for tomorrow," she said.

He nodded.

"I'm not leaving anything to chance. Hex is sending over schematics of Nonsuch Mansion and the grounds where the wedding will take place. Tomorrow morning, I'll meet with Killian and Bram to travel there." She smiled. "And you need to get your caterer's uniform."

Bennett snorted. "I'll have you know I had a job at a pub when I was a teenager."

"Really?" She could actually picture him behind a bar, smiling at the customers.

"Yes." He turned, driving along the Thames. Today the water was brown and murky. A tour boat with a glass roof chugged by. "I'm rather good at balancing trays of glasses."

"As far as I can tell, you're good at everything," she said. "Being a soldier, a boss, running a company."

Dull color filled his cheeks.

She grinned. "Are you blushing?"

"No." There was a growl to his voice.

"Don't worry, Mr. Knightley, I also know you can be gruff, bossy, and you're delightfully rough in bed."

He grunted. "Don't talk about sex, or I'll get hard." His rugged face turned serious. "I want this op to go off without a hitch. I want this Westley fucker in jail for Ajay's murder." A pause. "And I want you safe."

Warmth spread in her belly. "You know I can look after myself."

"I know that, but I'm still allowed to worry."

"Well, don't worry. I'm not concerned, because I know you'll have my back." Her nerves fluttered. "And Killian and Bram."

"I'll worry because I'm your man, and I don't want any part of you hurt."

She let out a laugh. "My man?"

He turned his head, his gaze intense. "Yes. After this is over, you and I will talk about us."

Hadley's nerves did a wild dance. He looked at her like he expected her to argue.

Be brave or a coward, Hadley Jane. Time to make a decision.

"Okay," she said carefully

"You agree?" His eyebrows winged up.

"Knightley, don't ruin the moment. I'll admit to feeling a little uneasy." *Freaked out, terrified.*

He grabbed her hand, a huge grin on his face. "It'll be fine, Hadley. I'm going to take good care of you, armor and all." But a second later his smile disappeared, and he looked in the rearview mirror.

"What's wrong?" she asked.

"A black Mercedes SUV has been following us for a while. I thought it was just a coincidence, but it's still with us and moving closer."

Hadley frowned, glancing in the side mirror. She saw the dark vehicle gaining on them.

They were still driving along the Thames, and traffic was thick.

"Can you lose them?"

"I can try," he said grimly.

Suddenly, a motorcycle swerved in front of them, almost grazing the Bentley. Bennett cursed and slammed on the brakes.

Hadley was thrown against the seat belt. She saw the rider glance at them. He was wearing a black helmet.

The SUV roared up right behind them.

Shit. "They've pinned us in." She leaned forward and

opened the glove box of the Bentley, unsurprised to find a SIG Sauer handgun. She grabbed it, checked it over, and slid the magazine in.

Bennett had pulled another handgun from the center console. It sat easily in his hand. His face was set, ready for a fight.

She watched the warrior come out.

There was a flash of movement out the side window. She turned her head.

And her entire chest turned to ice.

"Oh, fuck, Bennett. Brace!"

"What—?" He looked past her and cursed.

A garbage truck rumbled out of a side street, driving directly toward them.

Ahead, the biker pulled out a gun. Hadley guessed whoever was in the SUV was armed as well.

If they got out, they'd be gunned down.

There was no time to react anyway.

The garbage truck hit them. There was a crunch of metal and the Bentley rocked wildly, then started to slide.

Bennett was cursing steadily and threw an arm across Hadley's chest. The car kept sliding, pushed by the truck. A back window shattered.

Then the car slammed into the stone guardrail by the river.

Oh, God. She met Bennett's hazel gaze.

Then the railing gave way and the car rammed straight through it. There was a brief second of nothing, then they hit the water.

Quickly, faster than she'd thought possible, murky water filled the car.

"Belts off," he said sharply.

Hadley unsnapped hers. The water was rising fast. She tried to find her calm. She wasn't a huge fan of water. She was English, and wasn't a great swimmer. She liked the beach...when she was sitting on the sand sipping a cocktail.

"Hadley." A big hand gripped hers. The water was rising up past their chests. "I'll get you out."

Certainty filled her. She was with Bennett. "I know. Let's do this."

He gripped her chin, and pressed a quick, firm kiss to her lips.

The car kept sinking, the water reaching her mouth.

Then they both sucked in deep breaths, and the water completely filled the car, trapping them in a silent, murky world.

CHAPTER SIXTEEN

As the cold water closed over him, Bennett felt himself slip into battle readiness. It was a place where you let your worries and anxiety go, and focused only on the mission. On the primary objective.

Escape.

He needed to get Hadley to safety. He'd keep her safe, no matter what.

The car was sinking fast, and the water was dark. As soon as the vehicle was full, he tried to open the door, but it wouldn't budge.

Damn. The impact with the truck must have bent the frame.

He lifted his gun and slammed it against the window. He saw a crack. He slammed again and the tempered glass shattered.

Bennett lifted his legs and rammed a foot against the window, knocking the glass away.

He swam through the window, turned, and held a

hand out for Hadley. She was just a shadow in the front seat of the car, but then her fingers brushed his.

He pulled her out of the vehicle, and they kicked to the surface of the river. As soon as their heads broke the surface, relief hit him.

Thank God.

She was soaked, her hair plastered to her head. They both sucked in air.

"Bennett—"

Gunfire ripped through the air.

Bullets peppered the water around them.

Fucking hell. Adrenaline surging, Bennett yanked her under the water, kicking strongly. He still had his weapon in one hand, and he gripped her hard with his other. No one was hurting his woman.

They came up for air again, and he lifted his weapon. He kicked his legs to tread water and let his training take over. He saw the men standing at the railing of the river, guns aimed.

Bennett fired.

Bang.

Bang.

Bang.

He saw one gunman's head snap back. Another stumbled. The rest dived for cover.

"Under," Bennett yelled.

He and Hadley ducked under the water again, swimming to a new location. Then he stopped and came up again.

As he fired, he heard echoing shots beside him.

Hadley was calmly treading water and firing as well.

God, he loved her.

Hell of a time to realize he was in love with her.

Bullets whizzed close by, and he yanked Hadley against him, shielding her.

On the bank, he saw a big man launch himself at one of the gunmen.

"Come on." Bennett pulled her toward the edge.

They kicked and dived under again, swimming hard. Finally, they reached the rocky shore right at the edge of the river.

As they dragged themselves out of the water, he saw Cleopatra's Needle rising up nearby and stone steps leading from the water's edge. The Egyptian obelisk was flanked by the statues of two black sphinxes.

Ignoring the cold seeping into his bones, Bennett lifted his gun, and he moved up the stairs, dripping water. Hadley was right behind him.

He circled around the sphinx—

And came face-to-face with Henry, who also had a gun in his hand.

His best friend lowered his Glock. "Fuck."

Bennett lowered his SIG. "That's the word of the day."

"I took down a couple of the attackers." Henry scowled. "You and Hadley got a few of them too. They ran, and dragged their injured into an SUV and took off."

Bennett blew out a breath.

Then he turned, grabbed Hadley, and kissed her.

She slid a hand into his wet hair, and kissed him back.

"You two are okay then," Henry said dryly.

Bennett made himself pull back, but yanked Hadley against his chest, absorbing the feel of her.

This had to end. His enemy had to be stopped.

"How did you get here so fast?" he asked.

"I was on the way to the office on my bike." Henry nodded to the big, black motorcycle parked at the edge of the street.

The traffic was snarled, people milling around gawking, and he heard sirens in the distance.

"I got a ping on my phone that the Bentley was in an accident," his friend continued. "I probably broke a few traffic laws to get here."

Bennett clapped Henry on the arm. "I'm glad you did."

"Westley's getting desperate." Hadley wrapped her arms around her middle. "He's losing control." She met Bennett's gaze. "He wants to kill you."

Bennett stared at the abandoned garbage truck. "These guys will likely be hired mercenaries."

Hadley nodded.

He cupped the side of her face. Even soaking wet, she was beautiful.

"Well, I'm not really interested in dying." He looked up. "Henry, organize a car to pick us up. We'll go back to my place. Can you deal with the police?"

His friend nodded. "The press will work out that it's your car in the Thames."

"I think that's okay," Hadley said, a look in her eyes. "It provides good cover. Tell everyone that Bennett is recovering at home after a terrible accident."

Bennett nodded as well. "Westley will think that's where I am. Licking my wounds."

Henry glanced out over the river. "He won't be expecting you to be undercover as a caterer at a fancy wedding."

"Exactly."

"I'm coming tomorrow, by the way," Henry added.

Bennett frowned. "Henry—"

"I've already organized to join the MI6 crew."

"He's so darn clingy," Bennett muttered to Hadley.

She smiled, but then her nose wrinkled. "God, we smell bad."

"Yeah, I'm trying *not* to think about what's in the water." Bennett slung an arm over her shoulders. "Let's get out of here." He wanted to get her warm and dry.

He glanced again at the garbage truck and the destroyed railing. His jaw tightened.

Westley had almost hurt Hadley. That was unacceptable.

I'm coming for you, arsehole.

BENNETT GROANED, clamping his hands on Hadley's hips.

She rode him hard, moving up and down on his cock, her hands planted on his chest.

So damn beautiful.

Her hair was loose around her face, and the early morning light was making her skin glow. He'd stay here deep inside her for the rest of his damn life if he could.

He still wasn't sure he deserved her, but he planned to spend the rest of his life proving that he did.

"Get there, beautiful." He cupped one of her breasts.

She let out a throaty moan. "I love your cock, Bennett."

He groaned, and slid his hand down her flat belly. The way she was clenching on his cock, he wouldn't last much longer.

He found her clit. Damn, he loved watching the way she took him. Loved watching his cock sliding inside her.

"*Close*," she panted.

"Come," he growled.

She did. She threw her head back and cried out his name. Her pussy clamped down on him, and on the next upward thrust of his hips, he was coming.

"Hadley." His hands clenched on her hips, and he poured himself inside her.

She slumped over him. "Mmm."

He ran a hand over her back, savoring the feel of her.

"I need to get ready to go," she said.

His hand tightened on her. He knew that Killian was picking her up soon to head out to the country estate.

Tension threaded through his gut. It was going to be a lunchtime wedding—ceremony in the gardens if the weather permitted, followed by a long lunch.

After the accident yesterday, he and Hadley had holed up in his place and planned. They'd gone through every little detail of the wedding and the location. He glanced over at the white catering outfit resting on a chair in the corner of his room. He'd join the caterers shortly to drive out to Nonsuch Mansion in Surrey.

Hadley raised her head. "I can feel you tensing. It's going to be fine. We've got this."

"We've got no idea what Westley looks like, or what he has planned." So many things could go wrong. Bennett knew that because he'd had it happen before on missions.

Hell, just look at the one that had killed Hamed. His gut cramped.

She cupped his face, scratching his stubble. "We've *got* this. You, me, Killian, Bram, Henry, David and his guys. We'll be watching Kitty. We'll know when Westley makes contact, then we'll have him."

Bennett blew out a harsh breath.

She nipped his lips. "I promise we'll be back here this evening, fucking each other's brains out."

"Promise me, Hadley." He gripped her slim shoulders. "Promise you'll stay safe."

"What I will promise, Mr. Knightley, is that you won't be getting rid of me that easily."

He didn't want to get rid of her at all.

She climbed off. "Shower, food, and then I have to go."

They showered and ate together.

Then Bennett found himself standing in his bathroom, brushing his teeth beside Hadley. His heart squeezed. Yes, he wanted this. He wanted to start every morning together this way.

He also wanted to tell her that he was in love with her, but he knew it would unsettle her.

And she needed her focus for today's mission.

She rinsed her mouth and met his gaze in the mirror. "I need to hurry. Killian will be here soon."

She strode out and his gaze followed her. She wore black fitted trousers and a white shirt. No doubt she had another killer dress to wear to the wedding. She didn't look like a deadly security specialist.

But he knew. He knew every inch of her. She was as tough and smart as she was beautiful.

He couldn't let her get hurt today.

He lifted his chin and met his own gaze in the mirror, then he turned and followed her.

Hadley was flying around the living room, collecting her things. The place was cluttered with their prep from yesterday. Bennett had organized for a whiteboard to be delivered, and it was covered with a plan of the manor house and gardens. The coffee table was scattered with high-res photos of the place.

They were as ready as they'd ever be.

"I have something for you," he said.

She turned and raised a brow. "Another gift? Bennett, I don't need gifts all the time."

"I want you to take this one." He held up a slim, translucent vest.

She studied it and blinked.

"It's one of Secura's experimental, lightweight ballistic vests. It's so thin and light it fits under your clothes." He cleared his throat. "I had it made to your measurements. It'll mold to your body." It almost looked like a corset.

She walked up to him, went up on her toes, and kissed him. "Thank you."

She took the vest.

"I had a couple delivered to Killian's hotel for him and Bram as well."

Hadley pressed her hands to his chest. "It's going to be fine Bennett. The bad guy is going down today."

"Hell, yeah," he murmured.

She kissed him again. "See you at the wedding, Mr. Knightley."

"Count on it, Ms. Lockwood."

HADLEY TOOK Killian's hand and stepped out of the limo.

The weather had turned out spectacularly for the wedding. There was a blue sky overhead, the sun was shining, and the temperature was mild. She smiled at Killian. He looked mouthwateringly good in his fitted, black suit, bow tie, and white shirt. Sharp and handsome.

She straightened, and smoothed down her dress.

It had a sweetheart neckline, was blush pink with sparkly beading dotted on the bodice, as though someone had sprinkled the dress with glitter. The floor-length tulle skirt had a long split up one side.

Beneath the dress she wore the vest that Bennett had given her—it hugged her body tightly—and she had a small Smith & Wesson M&P Shield handgun strapped to her thigh. She knew Killian, Bram, and Bennett were wearing their vests too. She just hoped they didn't need them.

Her hair was up in an artful twist, and she wore the diamond earrings Bennett had given her.

It felt like he was with her.

She tucked her arm into Killian's.

"Nice pile," she murmured.

The historic house had long, elegant lines and was built in the Tudor style. She expected a Jane Austen character to pass by at any second.

"Henry VIII built Nonsuch Palace near here," Killian said. "It was destroyed, but this later mansion was built to echo its style."

"I didn't know you were so into British history, Killian."

"I was doing research for the mission."

"Sure." There was a huge green lawn, immaculate formal gardens that were just starting to flare to life, and less formal, wilder gardens that invited you to wander. They followed the line of wedding guests heading around the house to where chairs had been set up outside for the ceremony. There were huge urns of flowers everywhere.

The Wentworths had spared no expense for their son's wedding.

Hadley hoped the mission didn't ruin the wedding, but the first priority was catching Westley.

"Ooh, this place looks *fancy*." Hex's voice in her ear. "Does Bennett have a country estate?"

They were all wearing tiny earpieces. The translucent adhesives stuck to the skin behind the ear and were impossible to see.

"I don't have a country estate," Bennett said across the line. "But if Hadley wants one, I'll get one."

She heard Hex giggle, and Hadley rolled her eyes. She liked hearing his voice. She glanced toward the huge stone house. He was in there somewhere, with the catering team.

As they reached the back of the house, she saw a band setting up on the large terrace off the huge ballroom. A string quartet was playing near the chairs for the ceremony.

Hadley and Killian moved to take their seats. She saw a flash of dark red hair. Bram's large form dwarfed a chair in one of the middle rows. He looked around, his gaze sliding through them like he didn't know them.

She also knew that David's agents were sprinkled around. As she pretended to study the flowers, she also spotted Henry in a dark suit, flirting with a woman in a very short dress. The woman looked smitten.

"I love your dress, Hadley," Hex said.

"Thanks." She knew that Hex was tapped into the security cameras, including the extra hidden ones installed by the MI6 team the day before.

"There's Kitty," Killian murmured.

Hadley saw the woman at the front of the aisle, standing by an arch of flowers. The Wentworths stood side-by-side, and they looked very chilly with each other.

She guessed it wasn't fun discovering that your wife was rotten.

Kitty fidgeted, her hands clutching the skirt of her blue dress.

"She's going to give everything away," Hadley said.

"It's normal for the mother of the groom to be nervous," Killian replied.

"How many weddings have you been to?" Hadley asked.

"None. I'll have to go to my sister's sooner rather than later, and that'll be enough." He sounded less than happy about it, although she knew he respected his sister's partner, Camden.

They took their seats and scanned the crowd.

Now, all they needed was for Westley to make an appearance.

CHAPTER SEVENTEEN

S tanding in the doorway of the old mansion, Bennett listened to the swell of music from the string quartet.

The newly married couple beamed at each other as they walked back down the aisle, smiling and waving at their family and friends. They headed around to the terrace, their guests rising to follow.

He saw Kitty with her husband. The pair looked frigid.

Even though she couldn't see him, Bennett glared at the woman.

She'll be back behind bars soon.

First, they needed her to lead them to Westley.

Bennett looked around. No one in the crowd leaped out as being a criminal with a vendetta against Bennett.

Who the hell was it? What had Bennett ever done to deserve the havoc this bastard had wreaked.

Then he saw Hadley.

She was on the arm of Hawke, and Bennett's gut

tightened. Damn, they made a stunning couple, which he hated on principle.

She was in your bed this morning, making love with you.

That thought soothed him a little. He let his gaze run over her. The pink dress made him think of the first kiss of dawn. Did she have her vest on? His gaze lingered on the swell of her breasts.

She'd have it on. She'd known how important it was to him.

She lifted her head, spied him, then looked at him for a millisecond before looking away.

He watched her touch her earrings. The ones he'd given her.

Then she and Killian swept past to the terrace for drinks and the pre-lunch dancing.

Bennett straightened his white chef's jacket. He needed to get back to the kitchen and get his work done before he was missed. He really, really wanted to be out here searching for Westley, but he didn't want to ruin their chance of that happening.

As soon as Hadley spotted Westley, she'd let him know.

His hand clenched and unclenched. He stalked through the stately rooms, with their elegant wallpaper and artwork in huge gold frames.

As he walked, he heard the beautiful, stirring Air on the G String being played by the quartet.

And then the perfect image of Hadley walking down the aisle popped into his head.

He almost missed a step.

He could picture her clearly in a stunning white dress, love shining on her beautiful face as she walked toward him.

His chest tightened. *Hell.* He wanted that.

More than anything.

Maybe once this mess was over, he'd give his mum that summer wedding she dreamed about.

CRADLING A GLASS OF CHAMPAGNE, Hadley kept her gaze on Kitty.

The woman was down in the garden, talking with some guests. Unsurprisingly, her husband was on the other side of the gathering.

Hadley's shoulders were tense. She just wanted Westley to get here. She knew the waiting must be killing Bennett.

"Less frowning," Killian said. "This is supposed to be a happy occasion."

She looked back at Killian. "I'll be happy when Westley is in handcuffs."

"He will be. Soon."

She dragged in a steadying breath, and pretended to sip her champagne.

"The MI6 agents have all checked in," Hex said in their ears. "The perimeter of the estate is clear. No problems."

Hadley hoped the agents didn't scare Westley off. She knew David would've picked his best agents for the job. In fact, she knew most of them. She saw a couple of them now, chatting with some other guests. These people had no clue there were Secret Intelligence Service agents among them.

"Keep an eye on Kitty." Hadley set her champagne down. "I'm going to do a lap."

Killian gave her a bland look. "Tell Knightley I said hi."

She pulled a face at her boss, then made her way through the crowd. She saw the band pulling equipment out of huge black boxes and plugging instruments in. She skirted them and entered inside.

The ballroom was grand with parquet wood floors, wood paneling on the walls, chandeliers, and round tables overloaded with flowers. The scent of gardenias filled the air.

She strode onto a narrow hall. Rooms flanked it, most decorated in a stately style, with grand wallpaper and huge, framed mirrors on the wall. Soon, the sound of the wedding party faded, replaced by the low hubbub of voices and the tinkle of plates.

Her heels clicked on the wood floor as she made her way to the kitchen. She touched behind her ear to deactivate her earpiece.

She stopped in the doorway. The large kitchen was busy, and filled with caterers in white uniforms, zipping back and forth like bees on flowers.

A woman turned and spotted Hadley. "Oh? Are you lost?"

"Yes, sorry." Hadley spread her hands, a sheepish look on her face. "I seem to have taken a wrong turn on the way to the restrooms—"

A tall figure stepped in front of her. Bennett looked at Hadley politely, like she was a stranger, then the corner of his mouth tipped up. "I'll show you the way."

"Thank you," Hadley said.

He took her arm and led her out of the kitchen. Then he picked up speed, half dragging her down another corridor, then into an empty sitting room.

"You look bloody beautiful, Hadley." He backed her up until she hit the wall.

"You look kind of hot in that chef's outfit."

His mouth crashed down on hers. With a moan, she kissed him back, and bit his bottom lip.

She felt the tension in him, but also the ever-present desire.

"Don't mess me up," she panted.

He pressed his forehead to hers. "I want to." His hand found the slit in her dress, caressed her thigh, then brushed over her gun.

He groaned. "So sexy, Hadley."

She nipped his chin. "I need to get back, I just wanted to check on you."

"Well, I've diced about a thousand carrots, and plated about two hundred side salads."

She smiled. "It's good to learn new skills."

He cupped her ass through the skirt and squeezed. "You're asking for trouble, Ms. Lockwood."

"If you're the one giving it, I'll take it." She pressed one last kiss to his lips, then ducked around him. "I'd better get back."

"I hate that I'm on the other side of the bloody building and can't see what's going on," he grumbled.

"If you step out there, someone will spot you." She tapped her earpiece. "I'll keep you up to date."

"Hadley?"

She looked back over her shoulder. God, he was so handsome.

"Be careful," he told her.

There was so much emotion packed into his words.

She nodded, then she hurried back toward the party.

It was time to finish this.

She touched her ear. "Anything?"

"Kitty is still in the garden," Killian said. "She's alone at the moment. She just finished talking with some guests. It looks like the band will be starting soon."

"Watch her," Hadley said.

"Don't worry, I am." Her boss's voice was dry.

Right. Telling Killian "Steel" Hawke how to do his job wasn't exactly a good idea.

Hadley reached the doorway to the terrace. One of the band members was tuning a guitar. Guests were spread out across the terrace and gardens.

She stepped out, and instantly spotted Killian cradling a glass filled with amber fluid. She knew her boss liked a good bourbon or Scotch.

Down a set of mossy stone steps, Kitty was half hidden by a sculptured bush.

She was still alone.

But Hadley's senses were tingling. Her trouble radar was going off.

Then she turned her head. The five bandmembers were pulling more things out of the big, black boxes. The closest guy had a riot of tattoos up his arm.

She frowned. It didn't seem like the type of band the Wentworths would approve of.

Suddenly, a loud drumbeat started pounding out of the speakers. Hadley winced and saw guests turn to look.

Then her brain registered that the four men and one woman were no longer pulling instruments out of the boxes.

They were pulling out assault rifles.

Oh. Fuck.

"Everyone get down!" Hadley yelled above the thumping music. "They have guns!"

She ducked behind a table covered in glasses of champagne. She flipped it over, glasses smashing everywhere. "Killian, we have—"

Gunfire ripped across the terrace. Screams broke out. The loud music drowned most of it out.

Hadley ducked down behind the overturned table, and saw guests dropping to the ground. Nearby, one man was hit in the leg and collapsed.

Shit. *Shit.*

Hadley reached under her dress and pulled out her handgun.

"Five shooters. Four male, one female." Hex coolly rattled off their descriptions.

"Killian, don't lose Kitty," Hadley said.

"You just make sure you don't get killed," Killian barked. "I've got Kitty."

There was more gunfire. Shit, there were kids here.

Hadley popped up and fired. She clipped one man and he staggered.

She ducked back down, just as more gunfire ripped up the area around her.

Hell. She was pinned, and now they had her location. There were more shots. She peered to the side and saw Bram behind a stone wall, firing on the shooters. She spotted Killian standing nearby, gun up and aimed.

He wasn't in cover, like his own badassness would stop the bullets.

One gunman jerked, and she saw that the shot had hit him right between the eyes.

Damn, Killian was good.

More automatic gunfire sprayed the party, and wild screams erupted.

"They're not aiming to kill," Hadley said. "They're the distraction."

"Kitty is still crouched in the garden," Killian said.

Where are you, Westley?

Hadley tried to shift, but bullets peppered her hiding place, thudding into the thick table.

"Looks like you guys need a little help." The amused masculine voice cut across their earpieces.

Hadley froze. She didn't recognize the voice. *What the hell?*

"Who the fuck are you?" Hex snapped.

"The man who hacked your comms line, baby."

"What?" Hex sounded outraged. "No one hacks my line!"

"It wasn't easy," the man said, "but luckily I like a challenge."

"Who are you, motherfucker?" Hex demanded.

"Hmm, feisty. I like that too."

Hadley saw movement, a flash of red.

She swiveled her head and saw a woman in a long, red dress sprinting into the party.

Her dark red hair was pulled back in a slicked back hair style, and bold makeup accented her striking features.

Hadley gasped. She recognized the woman. The redhead leaped onto a table, ran along it, and lifted two large handguns.

She opened fire on the band.

Hadley heard Killian cursing across the line.

Then another man appeared. He wore a dark gray suit, and a black shirt with no tie. His dirty blond hair was pulled up in a man bun that added to his hotness.

He pulled a rifle and fired on the band as well, walking forward steadily.

He had a faint smile on his face.

"Get your ass into cover, Devyn," Killian snapped.

Hadley blinked. She'd never heard Killian use that tone of voice, or sound like he was so close to losing it.

"Nice to see you too, Steel." The redhead leaped off the table, ran, and slid in beside Hadley.

"Striker," the woman said with a nod.

"Hellfire," Hadley replied.

Devyn "Hellfire" Hayden was CIA, with a habit of turning up in the middle of tense operations.

Devyn's partner took out the final bandmember, then lowered his weapon. He sauntered over, a smile on his handsome face.

The way he moved made a woman think of sex. The hot, sweaty, and naughty kind.

Hadley and Devyn rose. Around them, guests were crying and screaming. A child wailed, and several people huddled around giving attention to the injured. The music continued to throb through the speakers.

"Hadley Lockwood, this is Shade," Devyn said.

Hadley jerked. She'd heard plenty of stories about the deep-cover CIA agent named Shade. The dangerous kind.

Killian appeared, his face was set in rigid lines. He was almost vibrating with anger. "What the hell are you two doing here?"

"You're welcome," Devyn said.

"We were tracking a mercenary group out of Romania," Shade said. "They got hired for this gig." The man jerked his head at the dead shooters. "We had no idea you were running an op until we got here."

"Killian, tell that jackass to get off my comm line!" Hex snapped.

A slow grin crossed Shade's face. "Is she as feisty as she sounds?"

"Where's Kitty?" Hadley asked.

"Bram has eyes on her," Killian said.

"And Bennett?" Hadley was half surprised he hadn't charged into the gun fight.

"The music covered the gunfight," Hex said. "The caterers don't know what's happened. I'll give him an update."

Hadley blew out a breath, then touched her ear. "Bram?"

"Wentworth is still in the garden," Bram replied. "Still alone. Wait." There was a pause and Hadley tensed. "Fuck, I can see her lips moving. She's talking to someone. I'm on the move. There might be someone on the other side of the hedge."

"Since you're here—" Killian looked at Devyn and Shade "—you two can help."

"Fuck!" Bram barked. "A man just ran from the gardens and into the crowd. He's in a blue suit, bald head, slim build. I've lost him."

"Fan out," Killian ordered.

Hyper focused, Hadley searched the crowd. Her heart pounded. *Where are you?*

Then she saw a man in a blue suit with a bald head run into the house.

"I saw him." Hadley broke into a sprint. "He's gone inside the house."

She ran through the doorway and gave chase.

CHAPTER EIGHTEEN

Hadley sprinted through the house. All the elegant rooms were empty.

Where did he go?

Then she heard girlish screams. She turned, following the sound, and sprinted down a wide hallway, her heels clicking fast.

She came out in a large room, and saw a bald man brandishing a gun at three young girls. They were the flower girls from the ceremony. They all wore white dresses, with wreaths of flowers in their hair.

No. *No.*

"Let them go." Hadley raised her weapon, aiming at the man's head.

He turned and she controlled her reaction. He was younger than she'd expected, but she saw now that he had no hair because of terrible scarring.

His head and half his face were covered in burn scars. One eye socket was empty, and the other had a shrewd brown eye.

"Stay back." His voice was raspy. "I have no problem shooting them."

"They aren't what you're after, Westley."

"No, they aren't." He swung his weapon toward Hadley. "Killing Bennett's whore would be much more satisfying." There was venom in his voice.

"Who are you?" she asked.

"The ghost of past sins." His voice was so scratchy that he had to have had some sort of throat trauma.

"You shoot, and I'll shoot," she said.

"Hmm, guess we have a standoff."

Suddenly, he moved. He grabbed one of the little girls. She shrieked and he shoved her at her friends.

Dammit. Hadley leaped in front of them to shield them.

Westley took off through a doorway. The girls were crying hysterically.

"It's okay. It's okay. Go." Hadley gave them a nudge. "Go in the opposite direction. Get outside."

The trio took off with stumbling steps, their dresses flaring around them.

Hadley sprinted after Westley. "Hex, can you see him?"

"I got a glimpse of him, Hadley. He's heading deeper into the house."

Where the hell was he going? She raced through a doorway, crossed a sitting room, and into another hallway.

"Oh, hell," Hex said. "Hadley, Killian spoke to Kitty. She told Westley that Bennett was with the caterers."

Hadley realized that he was heading for the kitchen.

For Bennett.

She picked up speed. "Warn Bennett that he's incoming."

"Acknowledged."

Bennett was *hers*. She wouldn't let this asshole hurt him.

She sprinted into the kitchen, only steps behind Westley.

He charged the catering stuff, knocking people out of his way. Shouts broke out. Plates fell, shattering on the floor and sending food splattering everywhere.

She leaped over the mess, running toward him. He aimed his gun at the ceiling and fired.

Panic ensued.

"Get down!" Hadley yelled.

She charged after the man. He rounded a bench, and Hadley saw a tall man in white dart out, a stack of plates raised over his head. Bennett slammed the plates down on Westley's head.

The bald man staggered and rammed into another bench, knocking glasses over. He caught himself, panting, and unfortunately still had his gun clutched in his hand.

Hadley raised hers, aiming at his chest.

"You all right?" Bennett asked her.

She nodded, her gaze darting between him and Westley.

Then Bennett swung back to look at the man.

She watched the color drain out of Bennett's face.

"*No.*" There was deep horror in his voice.

She felt ice slide into her veins.

Westley smiled, but it was humorless, tugging at his scars. "Hello, Bennett."

There was so much hate in those words.

"No. Paul. You're dead."

Paul? Hadley gripped the gun tighter. *Oh, God.*

The young SAS soldier who'd been killed in the same explosion as Hamed.

He'd been blown up, his body never recovered.

"I wish I was dead." Paul's face twisted. "There are things far worse than death."

She'd seen a photo of a young, blond man. He barely looked the same.

"I didn't die, Bennett. You left me!" Paul's voice rose. "You didn't save me. And they got me. The Taliban locked me up and tortured me." Paul's chest heaved.

"I'm sorry." Bennett's hands turned to fists, pain was stamped all over his face. "We thought you were dead."

"I wasn't. You were too busy with your precious Hamed. I know you brought him back here. You buried him here and brought his family here as well. They're cared for. Safe. Not like me."

Bennett took a step closer, and Paul waved his gun.

"Don't move or I'll kill you. I'll unload all my bullets into you."

Hadley watched the man carefully. This would cut Bennett deeply. He would never, ever abandon a man.

"I didn't know you were alive," Bennett said hoarsely.

"You brought Hamed and his family home, and you left me to rot." Paul lifted a hand and she realized it was prosthetic. "You left me burned and bleeding in the dirt, in agony. You left me for them. Do you know what they did to me? For months."

Bennett made a pained sound. "I'm so sorry, Paul. If I'd known, I'd have come for you."

"*Bullshit*. You left me. You came home, safe and sound, and made yourself billions of dollars." He spat the words.

"Paul—"

"*No*." The man shook his head wildly. "I've suffered pain you couldn't even imagine." His brown eye glittered and his gun swiveled toward Hadley. "And now you will too, Bennett."

"No." Bennett stepped toward her.

"I know you're fucking her. Let's see how you feel when she's dead."

Bennett's jaw clenched.

"Paul," Hadley said calmly. "I've got my gun aimed at you. If you shoot me, my bullet will kill you. I don't think you want to die."

"I don't care! All I want is to cause Bennett pain. To punish him."

"What happened to you was tragic. But Bennett isn't to blame." She knew he'd probably blame himself though.

"I'll make him suffer." Paul's chest shuddered as he took a breath. "But shooting you is too easy."

"Paul, please don't do this," Bennett said quietly. "I want more than this for you."

The younger man shook his head. "Life is pain, Bennett. Anyone who says differently is selling something."

Hadley straightened. She realized she'd heard those words before. *"The Princess Bride."*

"Very good." Paul nodded. "I wondered if Bennett would guess it was me when I used the code name Westley."

Taking a small step forward, Hadley didn't let her gun waiver. "Paul—"

"Enough." He swiveled the gun, aimed at Bennett, and fired three times.

No. No. No. The gunfire echoed in her ears, panic filling her.

She fired, but Paul moved, and she only clipped his arm. He cried out, slapping a hand over his bicep.

But all Hadley could see was Bennett falling.

THE PAIN HAD him gasping for breath.

Lying on his side, Bennett pulled in an agonizing breath. He felt like someone had taken a hammer to his chest.

His Secura vest had taken the brunt of the bullets, but it still hurt like hell.

"Bennett. God." Hadley's worried voice.

He pried his eyes open and saw Paul's legs.

A different pain seared through him. *Paul.* God, Paul. They'd left him. The Taliban had broken that funny young man who'd loved quoting movie lines.

He heard Hadley and Paul talking, but he couldn't quite make out the words. He needed air, and he needed the pain to stop before he could focus.

"Put your gun down," Paul ordered.

"Listen—" Hadley's voice.

"*Now*, or I'll put a bullet right between his eyes."

The sound of a scuffle.

Get up. Get up. But Bennett couldn't move yet. He managed to turn his head and saw Paul slapping handcuffs on Hadley's wrists

Fuck. No.

He tried to move, but the pain in his chest had nausea hitting him like a brick.

Paul was smiling, his single eye bright. "Yes, I have a much better idea on how to hurt him. I've tried to wreck his company, his people, spread rumors, but I think hurting you will cause him the most pain." Paul grabbed her arm.

Hadley's face was blank, but she watched her captor carefully.

"Let's go!" Paul jerked her out of view.

Dammit. Bennett forced his body to move. He rolled over onto his front, almost threw up from the pain, then saw the former soldier drag Hadley out the door.

Bennett forced back the nausea and pain with sheer will. He dragged himself across the floor.

He caught a glimpse of Paul pulling Hadley down the grass-covered slope at the back of the home, toward the trees.

Pain seared through his chest. He managed to sit up, and unbuttoned the chef's jacket. He leaned back against the wall.

Hadley could take care of herself for a bit. He tried to reassure himself. She'd wait for a chance to escape.

But sheer panic tasted metallic in his mouth.

Paul was determined to hurt Bennett. And the man had found the best way to do that.

Not happening.

Bennett touched his ear. "Kitchen. Help." He slumped.

He heard Hex's voice, but it was all a jumble.

He closed his eyes for a second, then he heard running footsteps.

"Fucking hell." Killian's voice.

Bennett opened his eyes and saw Killian crouching in front of him.

Behind the head of Sentinel Security stood Bram and Henry, and another couple. The stunning redhead looked familiar. That's right. She'd been in Italy when Bennett had brushed up against the Sentinel Security team. The tall, intense man with her had blond-brown hair pulled up in a bun.

"Who are they?" Bennett asked.

"Friends," Killian replied.

The pair were both clutching guns, so he hoped so. "He's got Hadley."

"What the hell happened, Bennett?" Henry crouched on the other side, worry on his face as he stared at the bullet holes in Bennett's shirt.

"Fuck, Henry. Westley...it's Paul. Paul Davies."

Henry sucked in a breath. "He's dead."

Bennett shook his head. Killian was loosening his vest and suddenly Bennett could breathe.

"It's Paul. He survived and was taken prisoner. He blames me."

"Christ." Henry scraped a hand over his head.

Bennett met Killian's gaze. "Paul wants to punish me. Everything he's done has been to hurt me."

Killian's face was grim. "Okay, let's get you on your feet."

Killian and Henry helped Bennett upright. His vision swam for a second, but the pain wasn't quite as bad now.

"Guys," Hex's voice in their earpieces. "Our bad guy must have a jammer. I can't contact Hadley."

"I need a weapon," Bennett said.

Henry frowned. "You should stay here—"

"No." He cut Henry off. "Paul has *my* woman. I'm not losing her."

The intense man with the tawny eyes and hair stepped forward, and held out a Glock to Bennett.

The man winked. "I'm a sucker for true love."

The redhead made a sound. "Since when?"

Bennett ignored them and checked the weapon. "He took her into the trees. She's handcuffed."

"He must have a vehicle close by," Bram said.

"Two teams," Killian said. "I'll go with Bennett and Henry. Bram, you're with Shade and Hellfire."

They all nodded and headed outside.

"Killian, I can confirm he took her into the woods heading south," Hex said. "I saw it from an exterior camera, but I've lost visual now."

"Acknowledged, Hex," Killian said. "We'll find her."

"Bring her home," Hex said.

Bennett blocked the stabbing pain in his chest and jogged toward the woods, flanked by Killian and Henry.

His mouth pressed into a flat line. He couldn't believe Paul was alive.

Damn. They'd left him. He suffered unimaginable horrors. Bennett had seen the results of torture over there.

Sorrow hit him.

If he'd known...

But he hadn't. He'd grieved for Paul and Hamed. He'd tried to make a difference with Secura in their honor.

No matter what he'd been through, Paul didn't get to come back and destroy other people's lives. Like he'd destroyed Archie, Ajay, and even Kitty Wentworth, just because he'd suffered so greatly.

And now Paul wanted to hurt Hadley in order to get back at Bennett.

That wasn't happening.

I'm coming, Hadley.

She'd hold on. His smart, beautiful woman would hold on.

The two teams split, Bram and the others circling around into the trees.

Then Bennett lifted his head and moved into a near silent run. *Time to get his woman back.*

CHAPTER NINETEEN

Hadley stumbled behind Paul, trying to slow him down.

Whatever he'd been through had broken him—and a part of her felt sympathy for him.

But he'd fixated on Bennett as the one to blame, and that, she wouldn't allow.

She knew that Bennett would already tear himself up that they hadn't realized Paul was still alive, that he'd been held captive and tortured.

Hadley wasn't going to let this shattered man use her as a tool to hurt the man she loved.

God. She loved Bennett Knightley so much.

"Hurry up," Paul snapped. He grabbed a handful of her dress and yanked.

She stumbled. "I'm going as fast as I can with my hands cuffed like this." She held them up. "Plus I'm in high heels."

He made a disgruntled sound and jerked her again. "Just keep moving."

Hadley followed, purposely tripping and stumbling. She couldn't help but worry about Bennett. This asshole had shot him three times. She knew he was in a vest, but vests weren't foolproof, and the impact of three bullets would still hurt.

He'll be fine. He's tough and strong.

She blew out a breath.

And he'd come for her.

She felt a rush of rock-solid assurance. Bennett Knightley would crash through any obstacle to get to her.

She trusted him more than she'd ever trusted anyone.

"If Bennett had known you were alive, Paul, he would've come for you."

"Shut up."

"I think you know that. You're angry, in pain, and there is no one to blame except the bad guys who hurt you."

He growled, sounding like a wounded animal.

"I was burned from the blast and my hand amputated. They took me. I was in agony. They only gave me minimal medical attention." His voice vibrated with emotions. "The pain was so bad that I wanted to die. For a while, I was sure Bennett and the team would come." Now his words turned to a broken whisper. "But they never did. I still remember the day I accepted that no one was coming."

Hadley's heart hurt for him.

"Once I was well enough, the torture started. They wanted intel. The things they did..." He stopped, staring into the trees.

"Paul, Bennett will help you. He'll get you help—"

"No! It's too late. I escaped those bastards, blowing up as many as I could. I want vengeance. That's all that's left for me."

"Do you really think that hurting Bennett will make you feel better?"

"Yes." His head whipped around, a resolute look in his eye, along with a hint of desperation.

Maybe deep down he knew it wouldn't soothe his pain, but he'd fixated on Bennett and he wasn't letting go.

Paul jerked her close and she felt the wash of his hot breath on her cheek.

"Hurting you will break him." Paul's voice was low now, a sly undertone. There was no sign of the man she'd felt sympathy for a moment ago. "He'll be broken like me. Maybe I'll kill you now." He lifted the handgun and pressed it under her jaw. "Maybe I'll leave your dead body here in the trees for him to find."

Hadley tensed, ready to fight. She wouldn't go down easily.

Then Paul smiled, his lips twisting. "No." He lowered the gun. "I want him to know I've got you, that I'm hurting you. I want to prolong his suffering."

Whoever Paul had been before was gone. She kept her gaze on his.

Then he jerked his head. "Come on."

They'd just taken two steps when there was a rustling noise to their left.

Paul froze. A second later, Hadley saw a deer walk out of the bushes. It raised its head, spotted them, then took off running.

Her captor shoved her ahead of him.

"Where are we going?" she asked.

"I have a car parked on a country road."

Shit. She couldn't let him get her in a vehicle.

Come on, Bennett.

She knew Killian and the others would be with him. They'd come.

But would they be in time?

She'd avoided romantic relationships for so long. Casper had left her unwilling and unable to trust.

Now, more than anything, she wanted the chance.

She wanted Bennett by her side. She had no idea how they'd work it out, with her in New York and him in London, but they would.

The trees thinned, and then she saw a wooden fence line.

Oh, crap. They'd reached the edge of the estate.

She had to stop Paul.

She pulled in a slow breath.

He turned away from her toward the fence, and she sprung.

Hadley got her cuffed hands over his head. She yanked back, the metal pushing against his throat.

He made an enraged sound, reaching back to try and grab her.

She yanked harder, and he choked. Then he jabbed an elbow back, catching her in the face.

Ow, dammit.

Her hold loosened and he tried to turn. They whirled and hit a tree. He was stronger than he looked.

"*Bitch.* You bitch."

Another ungainly turn, and they tripped and fell on the ground.

It was muddy and covered in rotting leaves. They rolled again, both of them fighting for control.

Hadley used all her strength to try and choke him.

His next elbow hit her in the gut, slamming into her vest, but she still felt the power behind it.

He grabbed her thigh through her dress and squeezed hard.

She hissed. God, it hurt. She scissored her legs.

But she knew he was too strong. She couldn't hold him off much longer.

Bennett. Her thoughts turned to him.

Then she saw him burst out of the trees like a vision.

She blinked. No, he was very real.

He charged forward. "It's over, Paul."

Paul jerked and made an animalistic noise. He elbowed Hadley again and she grunted.

A gunshot echoed through the trees and Paul yelped.

There was a flurry of movement and voices. She saw Killian and Henry, guns in their hands.

Then Bennett was there, untangling her from Paul.

Bennett pulled her into his arms. "Thank God." His voice was shaky.

"I knew you'd come."

"Are you hurt?" He touched her cuffed wrists. They were red.

"I'm fine." She cupped his cheek, saw the whites of his eyes. "Bennett, I'm fine."

Some of the panic leaked from him. His gaze ran over her face, then he pulled her close.

Leaning into his hard chest, Hadley looked at Paul. The man was sprawled on the ground, panting, a hand pressed to his bleeding leg.

"We'll get you help, Paul," Bennett said.

"*No*. I only want your pain, Bennett. I want you to suffer the way I've suffered."

Suddenly, Paul pulled another gun from under his shirt.

Bang.

Hadley jerked. Paul hadn't even lifted his weapon. Killian stood nearby, gun steady and face cool. Paul was slumped on the ground. The shot had hit him between the eyes.

"It's over," she whispered.

Bennett nodded, but he was stiff. She pressed her face into his neck. His skin felt like ice. She pressed closer and held on.

IT WAS LATE when Bennett let Hadley into his penthouse. After the chaos of the wedding, it'd taken some time to set things straight.

The injured had been taken to hospital. The shocked guests were calmed down. Shade and Hellfire had melted back into the shadows, and Kitty was back in custody. The bodies of the dead mercenaries and Paul had been taken away.

They'd left David to deal with the rest of the cleanup.

Bennett had stood over Hadley while a paramedic

had checked her out. After some ice on her cheekbone, she'd insisted that she was fine. She'd wanted him to go to the hospital to get his torso checked, but he'd refused.

She was still in her pink dress, the skirt of it smeared with dirt and mud.

She was the most beautiful thing he'd ever seen.

"Lights on." He dropped his keys on the hall table.

He was numb right now. He felt like he was made of ice inside. It had started spreading from the moment he'd realized who Westley was.

Seeing Paul alive, knowing what had happened to him... Bennett's chin dropped to his chest. Paul had been a part of Bennett's team, and Bennett had failed him.

He pulled in a shuddering breath.

I hope you've found your peace now, Paul.

And Bennett hoped, in time, he could work through everything that happened and accept it.

Warm hands cupped his cheeks. "Bennett?"

Hadley's beautiful face was in front of him, worry in her eyes.

"I'll be okay," he said. "Eventually."

"Talk to me. How do you feel?"

"Numb. Cold inside. Paul..."

"It's terrible what happened to him. But he was wrong to blame you. And everything he did was wrong. You can't purge your pain by inflicting it on others."

Bennett slid his arms around her. "How do you purge it?"

"It takes time." She leaned closer, her breasts pressed to his chest. "It takes leaning on others who care about you. It takes mulling it over and putting all the pieces together the best you can. It takes love."

His heart thumped hard.

"Now, I'm going to take care of you, Mr. Knightley." She took his hand in hers, and pulled him toward the bedroom.

In his bathroom, she unbuttoned his shirt and pushed it off. She helped him remove his vest and he shoved his trousers off.

He stood there in black boxer briefs, and saw her stare at his chest and sucked in a breath.

The bruises weren't pretty.

"I'm alive," he reminded her.

She nodded. "I hated watching him shoot you." She leaned forward and pressed gentle kisses over the bruising. "When he had me, I knew you were coming for me. I know you'll always come."

His hands clenched on her hips. "Always, Hadley."

"You would've rescued Paul if you'd known he was alive."

"Of course, I would." Something loosened in his chest. He would never have given up.

"My protector," she murmured. "You can't help but save people. Now, you just do it by giving them jobs."

She was determined to see the best in him. "Hadley—"

She pressed her mouth to his. The kiss was deep, filled with love and longing. He pulled her closer with a groan.

Inside, he felt the numbness cracking. Emotion—

everything he felt for this woman—was warming him up, bringing him back to life.

"I need you," he murmured against her lips.

"I'm here. Take whatever you need."

He wanted to hurry. To ravage and take.

Instead, he forced himself to move slowly.

He pushed the straps of her dress off her shoulders. Her slim torso was encased in the vest he'd given her. She looked like a queen in armor.

He unclasped it and slid it off her. Beneath was a tiny, sheer bra and it was gone in seconds.

He pushed the dress down over her hips, and then shoved her panties down her legs. Slender but so strong. So beautiful.

He ran his hands down her sides. *His.* He'd never, ever get enough of her. He dropped a kiss to her shoulder, then moved his mouth up her neck. She made a husky sound.

Then Bennett nudged her into the shower.

They took their time washing each other. He stroked her soapy skin, touching her everywhere.

She did the same to him, ratcheting his need for her higher and higher.

Bennett was no longer cold or numb.

He was an inferno inside. And Hadley was both the fuel and the flame.

He couldn't hold back any longer. He turned her, and pressed her palms against the wall. He smoothed a hand over her arse and pressed close. His hard cock brushed between her legs and he groaned. He scraped his teeth along her shoulder.

"I love you, Hadley."

She gasped. She looked back over her shoulder and met his gaze.

"You're mine, and I'm not letting you go. And I'm not letting you run. If you do, there's nowhere you can hide where I won't find you." His voice was almost a growl.

She smiled. "Then it's very lucky I love you too, Mr. Knightley."

Elation flared inside him.

"I want you," she said. "I want everything, Bennett."

"I'll give you everything. You already have my heart."

"That's all I need."

He pushed inside her, and they both groaned. That tight, slick feel of her sent his senses into overdrive.

He pulled back, then started thrusting.

Hadley pushed herself back on his cock, her breathy cries filling his ears.

He slid a hand under her wet, straining body and found her clit. He rubbed in firm circles.

Her cries changed. She was close.

And pleasure was a hot clamp on his gut. "Hadley. My beautiful Hadley." He thrust faster.

"Yes, Bennett. *Please*."

All he could hear was the roar in his ears. Then she came, moaning his name, her body squeezing his cock.

With two more desperate thrusts he came.

"Damn, Hadley." His cock swelled. Pleasure pulsed as his climax crashed through him. He held her tight, coming inside her.

Wrecked, he pressed harder against her. He wanted to stay connected to her. He slid a hand into her wet hair.

"*Mmm.*" She pressed into his palm. "I really love you, Mr. Knightley."

"I love you too, Ms. Lockwood."

He spun her. The next kiss was sweet, and filled with trust and love.

CHAPTER TWENTY

Hadley loved shopping. It was her weakness.

It wasn't about spending money or adding to her wardrobe. What she loved was finding the perfect outfit, for herself or someone else, to suit the occasion. A perfect reflection of them.

She looked in the large window of an exclusive menswear store on Regent Street. That sweater was the perfect shade of green to match Bennett's hazel eyes. Plus the cashmere would drape over his muscled chest just right.

She smiled. She had to get it. She turned toward the door.

"No. No more." Bennett closed in, holding all her shopping bags. "We're done."

"Just one more."

"No. You've been into a hundred shops already."

It was three days after the wedding. Three days since they'd finished their mission.

Kitty Wentworth was in custody and would go to

trial for her crimes. Archie Martin was getting the best treatment Bennett could find. Ajay Patel would be laid to rest on the weekend.

Paul had already had a quiet burial arranged by Bennett. He'd had no family left, so it had only been Bennett, Hadley, and Henry in attendance.

Bennett had been quiet afterward, and spent some time after the funeral brooding. But he'd be fine. She'd make sure of it.

They'd spent the rest of their time having exceptional sex. She'd done her best to distract him and spoil him a little. And she had a lot more planned.

A lifetime of it.

She felt a little niggle in her belly, but pushed it away. She wasn't letting the past dictate her life anymore. She was in love with Bennett. She wasn't afraid of that.

Most of that niggle of worry was because she didn't want to leave Sentinel Security, yet Bennett had responsibilities with Secura here in London. It was an obstacle, but not an insurmountable one. Or that's what she kept telling herself. Still, he hadn't brought the subject up. Not even when Killian and Bram had flown back to New York yesterday. Her boss had given her a week off to recover and sort things out.

She pressed her hands to Bennett's chest and kissed him. "One more shop. I want to get something for you."

He jiggled the bags. "Half of these are for me."

"You deserve them." She nipped his lips.

He slid a hand along her cheek. "I'm okay, beautiful. I promise."

She smiled. "I know."

God, he looked handsome. After the mild weather of the weekend, the British weather had changed its mind. It was cold again. She was wrapped in her favorite camel-colored coat, while Bennett wore a navy-blue three-quarter length coat that looked hot on him.

"All I want is you," he murmured.

"Well, luckily you've got me."

He slid an arm around her and cupped her ass. "By the way, I'm planning on buying you a country estate."

She groaned. "I don't need a country estate."

"And I'm getting you a Bentley Continental GT. I know you liked it."

"I don't need a car either."

"And I'll never stop getting you more jewelry."

Her nose wrinkled. "I won't say no to all the jewelry. Within limits." A woman was only so strong.

"Soon, that jewelry is going to include a ring." He grabbed her left hand and her chest hitched. "I know we don't have all the logistics worked out yet." He stroked her ring finger. "But I can't wait to declare to the world that you're mine."

Her heart melted. "Bennett."

He kissed her, pedestrians flowing around them.

"Hadley?" a female voice clipped.

They pulled back, and Hadley suppressed a groan. "Mother."

She saw both her mother and father standing there. As always, they were impeccably dressed. Her father was in a gray suit, and her mother was wearing a long, olive-green dress and a black coat. They'd clearly been at some sort of appointment.

"I didn't expect to find you...cavorting on the street." Her mother's disapproval was clear. Like Hadley had been having naked sex in the gutter.

She suppressed an eye roll. "It's called kissing, Mother. It's perfectly legal, and people do it all the time."

"You've been avoiding my calls," her mother said frostily.

Hadley sighed. "I've been working."

"And are you working now?"

"Mother—"

"Really, carrying on like this in public is unseemly, Hadley."

Hadley didn't really care. Her parents' opinions had ceased to truly matter to her a long time ago.

She was happy. She was good at her work, had great friends, and now a man who loved her. She didn't care what they thought.

"I'm sorry, Mrs. Lockwood." Bennett stepped forward. "It's partly my fault."

He was all smooth manners, but Hadley saw the dark glint in his eyes. He was ready to protect her.

She took his hand and smiled.

Her mother frowned and opened her mouth.

But Hadley's father spoke first. "You're Bennett Knightley."

"What?" Hadley's mother frowned. "The billionaire?"

"It's a pleasure to meet you both," Bennett said. "Hadley's very important to me."

"Hadley..." Her mother's voice changed. "You snagged a billionaire."

Hadley felt a sour feeling invade her belly. "He's not a fish, Mother."

"It's *very* good to see you finally making a good decision, Hadley," her father said. "Knightley, I'm sure you can convince our girl to stop playing games with this work of hers and move home."

Hadley rolled her eyes, then felt a pulse of something from Bennett. *Uh-oh.* He looked angry.

"Hadley's very good at her job. She's smart, talented, and skilled. You should both be proud of her. She saves lives. What do you do?"

Hadley's mother gasped. Her father scowled.

"She's the most amazing woman I've ever met," Bennett continued. "She cares. She's selfless. She's protective. And I'm totally in love with her."

Hadley turned to goo inside. She smiled up at him. "I totally love you too."

He pulled her close. "By the way, I'm moving to New York."

She blinked. "What?"

"I know you love Sentinel Security."

"But Secura—"

"I'm going to open a US office in New York."

Her heart filled. "Really?"

"Really." He cupped her jaw. "I told you that I'd always give you everything you wanted, beautiful."

She kissed him, totally forgetting about her parents, the busy street, the cold weather.

It was just her and Bennett.

Right then, she didn't need anything else.

One month later

AT THE END of a long day, Bennett walked out of the elevator into the Sentinel Security office.

He'd spent most of the day at the future Secura New York office. It was currently being outfitted, and recruitment was underway for staff members. Maudie and Henry were helping him.

Henry deciding to join Bennett in New York hadn't been a surprise, but when Maudie declared that she was coming too, he'd been shocked.

"You wouldn't last a second without me," she told him with a sniff. "Your schedule would be all messed up."

Secretly, he'd been pleased. Clearly her grumpiness had grown on him.

In the Sentinel Security office, he walked past an exposed brick wall, then a green wall covered in plants. He was eager to see his woman.

Ahead, he heard the murmur of voices. He strode under the archway into Hex's lair. The giant interactive screen was filled with information. He'd ordered a screen just like it for the Secura office.

Bram and Matteo "Hades" Mancini stood with their arms crossed, reading the screen.

Hex spotted him. She had a small earpiece resting on one ear. "Hottie billionaire, you're looking fine today."

"Right back at you, hottie hacker."

She grinned. Her hair had extra pink streaks in it today. She wore jeans and a green T-shirt with the

Android logo on the front of it. The Android robot eating the Apple logo.

"Knightley," Bram rumbled.

Bennett lifted his chin at the man.

"How's your new office?" Matteo asked.

"Coming along. Painters are busy in there. I wanted to see if you guys were keen for some after-work drinks."

He was trying to make a habit of not working long hours, and going out for drinks at least once a week.

It was easy to do now that he had Hadley to come home to.

"I am." Hex raised her hand. "We've hit a wall with the current case. I've got searches set up to run overnight."

"I'll call Gabbi," Matteo said. "She's out running down something for another case."

"Nick and Lainie?" Bennett asked. Over the last few weeks, he'd become good friends with all the Sentinel Security members and their partners.

"On a jet to Chicago," Hex said. "Lainie has some deal on, so Nick tagged along."

Bram made a sound. "Man can't stay away from her." He cleared his throat. "I can't make it." The man looked even more unhappy than usual. "I have...stuff." He ambled out.

Hex stared after Bram. "Something is really wrong with him. I've asked him what's bothering him, but all I get is a grunt."

Matteo gripped her shoulder and squeezed. "He'll share when he's ready."

"And where's my lovely girlfriend?" Bennett asked.

"In Killian's office," Hex said. "They're talking with MI6 about something. They should be almost finished."

Bennett headed that way, but Hadley strode out, saw him and smiled.

"Hello, Mr. Knightley."

"Hello, Ms. Lockwood." He dropped a kiss to her mouth. "I missed you today." He breathed in her citrus and floral perfume.

She fiddled with the collar of his shirt. "I missed you too. Everything good at the office?"

He nodded. "We're heading for drinks with the gang."

"Sounds good. Then I recall I promised you a cooking lesson tonight."

He nipped her earlobe. "Only if my teacher is wearing that bodysuit I got her last week."

"Bennett, it's little more than a ribbon and two strips of silk."

"I know. I can't wait to see you in it." Then take her out of it, and touch her, kiss her, make her scream his name.

She shook her head, but she was smiling, so he figured the odds were in his favor.

He'd moved into her apartment here in the Sentinel Security warehouse. He'd added a few things of his own, but he liked her place and her style. It felt like home.

Really, as long as Hadley was there, he was happy.

He had bought her the Bentley, though. She'd protested, but he knew she loved it.

She'd also taken him to Nightingale House for a visit. Many of the residents had been cautious of him, uncertain around a man. But sweet Cora hadn't been. She'd been giddy that Hadley had a boyfriend.

He hadn't mentioned to Hadley yet that he'd made a rather large donation to the shelter in her name. She'd get exasperated at him, but she'd be happy about it.

He was so damn happy.

Every now and then, he thought of Paul and it hurt. Such a damn waste. He felt the same when he thought of Ajay and Archie.

But life moved on.

Just yesterday, Hamed's little girl had sent him a drawing of the New York skyline. Telling him that she missed him, and she hoped he was having a good time. He smiled. Hamed would be proud of her, and the bright future she had ahead of her.

And he'd be proud that Bennett was living his life.

He was seizing life and living it to the fullest with Hadley, in honor of those he'd lost.

"Did I hear someone mention drinks?" Killian appeared, buttoning his suit jacket.

"Yeah," Bennett said. "I'll buy you a Balvenie, Killian."

"I'd prefer a Pappy Van Winkle bourbon."

"Done."

"The 23-year-old."

Which didn't come cheap but was a decent drop. "I think I can afford it."

As they headed back to the others, they heard an enraged shriek.

"That asshole! He just hacked my tablet."

They saw Hex waving a hand in the air, her face red.

"I *cannot* believe him."

"Someone hacked the Sentinel Security system?" Killian's face looked like thunder.

"No." Hex took a breath. "No one can get through the Sentinel Security firewall. It's my personal tablet."

"Who?" Killian demanded.

"Fucking Shade." Hex tapped and swiped on her tablet. "He likes playing games. You'd think a spy would, you know, be busy with more important things." Her gaze narrowed. "I'll get him back."

Bennett glanced at Hadley, and saw her hiding a smile.

"What did he say?" Hadley asked.

Hex's cheeks pinkened. "Nothing interesting."

"Spill, Adler," Hadley demanded.

"He complimented me on the challenge of getting into my system." She tossed her head back. "He said he likes...sliding into tight places."

Matteo broke into laughter.

"Matteo!" Hex cried. "Your phone will stop working if you aren't careful."

Killian cleared his throat. "Shade plays by his own rules."

"Oh, I know." Hex looked right at Killian. "He also said to tell you that he hasn't heard from Hellfire."

Killian frowned. "What?"

"She was supposed to check in twenty-four hours ago, but she didn't. Shade said if you hear from her, to let him know."

With a muttered curse, Killian headed back toward

his office. "I'll meet you guys at the bar. I need to make a few calls first."

Bennett watched the man go. "Only a man with nerves of steel could take on that redhead."

Hadley smiled. "I know."

Hex glared at her tablet. "I'll give Shade a challenge, the asshole."

"Come on, Hex, I'll buy you a cocktail," Bennett said.

"Or three," the hacker replied.

As everyone gathered their bags and jackets, Bennett pulled Hadley aside.

"I got you something."

"Bennett." Her voice was exasperated. "You got me lingerie last week."

He held up a long, narrow box and opened it. The bracelet was made of shining platinum, with a heart pendant jewel attached. It was a light blue.

She sighed. "It's beautiful."

"It's the color of your eyes. It signifies that you hold my heart."

She shook her head, love in her eyes, and held out her hand. He fastened it on her slender wrist.

"It's beautiful. Is it topaz or aquamarine?"

"Um..."

"Bennett. Dammit, it's a sapphire, isn't it? It must have cost a fortune."

He decided to stay quiet since it was a blue diamond. It also matched the stone he was going to have made into her engagement ring.

He might keep that bit to himself for now.

"I love you, Ms. Lockwood." He pulled her close.

"I love you too, Mr. Knightley."

He pressed his mouth to hers. "Never letting you go."

"Then it's a good thing I never want you to let me go."

"Drinks!" Hex yelled. "Stop canoodling, you two, I need a cocktail."

With a laugh, Bennett tucked Hadley under his arm and followed their friends.

I hope you enjoyed Hadley and Bennett's story!

Sentinel Security continues with *Steel*, starring Killian "Steel" Hawke (yes, it's Killian's turn!) and a certain redheaded CIA agent. Coming January 2023.

For more action-packed romance, and to learn about when Monroe O'Connor first cracked a Rivera safe, check out the first book in the **Billionaire Heists**, *Stealing from Mr. Rich* (Monroe and Zane's story). **Read on for a preview of the first chapter.**

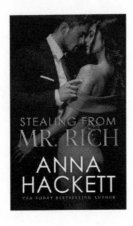

Don't miss out! For updates about new releases, free books, and other fun stuff, sign up for my VIP mailing list and get your *free box set* containing three action-packed romances.

Visit here to get started: www.annahackett.com

Would you like a FREE BOX SET of my books?

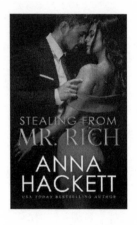

Brother in Trouble

Monroe

The old-fashioned Rosengrens safe was a beauty.

I carefully turned the combination dial, then pressed closer to the safe. The metal was cool under my fingertips. The safe wasn't pretty, but stout and secure. There was something to be said for solid security.

Rosengrens had started making safes in Sweden over a hundred years ago. They were good at it. I listened to the pins, waiting for contact. Newer safes had internals made from lightweight materials to reduce sensory feedback, so I didn't get to use these skills very often.

Some people could play the piano, I could play a safe. The tiny vibration I was waiting for reached my fingertips, followed by the faintest click.

"I've gotcha, old girl." The Rosengrens had quite a few quirks, but my blood sang as I moved the dial again.

I heard a louder click and spun the handle.

The safe door swung open. Inside, I saw stacks of jewelry cases and wads of hundred-dollar bills. *Nice.*

Standing, I dusted my hands off on my jeans. "There you go, Mr. Goldstein."

"You are a doll, Monroe O'Connor. Thank you."

The older man, dressed neatly in pressed chinos and a blue shirt, grinned at me. He had coke-bottle glasses, wispy, white hair, and a wrinkled face.

I smiled at him. Mr. Goldstein was one of my favorite people. "I'll send you my bill."

His grin widened. "I don't know what I'd do without you."

I raised a brow. "You could stop forgetting your safe combination."

The wealthy old man called me every month or so to open his safe. Right now, we were standing in the home office of his expensive Park Avenue penthouse.

It was decorated in what I thought of as "rich, old man." There were heavy drapes, gold-framed artwork, lots of dark wood—including the built-in shelves around the safe—and a huge desk.

"Then I wouldn't get to see your pretty face," he said.

I smiled and patted his shoulder. "I'll see you next month, Mr. Goldstein." The poor man was lonely. His wife had died the year before, and his only son lived in Europe.

"Sure thing, Monroe. I'll have some of those donuts you like."

We headed for the front door and my chest tightened. I understood feeling lonely. "You could do with some new locks on your door. I mean, your building has top-notch security, but you can never be too careful. Pop by the shop if you want to talk locks."

He beamed at me and held the door open. "I might do that."

"Bye, Mr. Goldstein."

I headed down the plush hall to the elevator. Everything in the building screamed old money. I felt like an imposter just being in the building. Like I had "daughter of a criminal" stamped on my head.

Pulling out my cell phone, I pulled up my accounting app and entered Mr. Goldstein's callout. Next, I checked my messages.

Still nothing from Maguire.

Frowning, I bit my lip. That made it three days since I'd heard from my little brother. I shot him off a quick text.

"Text me back, Mag," I muttered.

The elevator opened and I stepped in, trying not to worry about Maguire. He was an adult, but I'd practically raised him. Most days it felt like I had a twenty-four-year-old kid.

The elevator slowed and stopped at another floor. An older, well-dressed couple entered. They eyed me and my well-worn jeans like I'd crawled out from under a rock.

I smiled. "Good morning."

Yeah, yeah, I'm not wearing designer duds, and my bank account doesn't have a gazillion zeros. You're so much better than me.

Ignoring them, I scrolled through Instagram. When we finally reached the lobby, the couple shot me another dubious look before they left. I strode out across the marble-lined space and rolled my eyes.

During my teens, I'd cared about what people thought. Everyone had known that my father was Terry O'Connor—expert thief, safecracker, and con man. I'd felt every repulsed look and sly smirk at high school.

Then I'd grown up, cultivated some thicker skin, and learned not to care. *Fuck 'em.* People who looked down on others for things outside their control were assholes.

I wrinkled my nose. Okay, it was easier said than done.

When I walked outside, the street was busy. I smiled, breathing in the scent of New York—car exhaust, burnt meat, and rotting trash. Besides, most people cared more about themselves. They judged you, left you bleeding, then forgot you in the blink of an eye.

I unlocked my bicycle, and pulled on my helmet, then set off down the street. I needed to get to the store. The ride wasn't long, but I spent every second worrying about Mag.

My brother had a knack for finding trouble. I sighed. After a childhood, where both our mothers had taken off, and Da was in and out of jail, Mag was entitled to being a bit messed up. The O'Connors were a long way from the Brady Bunch.

I pulled up in front of my shop in Hell's Kitchen and stopped for a second.

I grinned. *All mine.*

Okay, I didn't own the building, but I owned the store. The sign above the shop said *Lady Locksmith*. The logo was lipstick red—a woman's hand with gorgeous red nails, holding a set of keys.

After I locked up my bike, I strode inside. A chime sounded.

God, I loved the place. It was filled with glossy, warm-wood shelves lined with displays of state-of-the-art locks and safes. A key-cutting machine sat at the back.

A blonde head popped up from behind a long, shiny counter.

"You're back," Sabrina said.

My best friend looked like a doll—small, petite, with a head of golden curls.

We'd met doing our business degrees at college, and had become fast friends. Sabrina had always wanted to be tall and sexy, but had to settle for small and cute. She was my manager, and was getting married in a month.

"Yeah, Mr. Goldstein forgot his safe code again," I said.

Sabrina snorted. "That old coot doesn't forget, he just likes looking at your ass."

"He's harmless. He's nice, and lonely. How's the team doing?"

Sabrina leaned forward, pulling out her tablet. I often wondered if she slept with it. "Liz is out back unpacking stock." Sabrina's nose wrinkled. "McRoberts overcharged us on the Schlage locks again."

"That prick." He was always trying to screw me over. "I'll call him."

"Paola, Kat, and Isabella are all out on jobs."

Excellent. Business was doing well. Lady Locksmith specialized in providing female locksmiths to all the single ladies of New York. They also advised on how to keep them safe—securing locks, doors, and windows.

I had a dream of one day seeing multiple Lady Lock-smiths around the city. Hell, around every city. A girl could dream. Growing up, once I understood the damage my father did to other people, all I'd wanted was to be respectable. To earn my own way and add to the world, not take from it.

"Did you get that new article I sent you to post on the blog?" I asked.

Sabrina nodded. "It'll go live shortly, and then I'll post on Insta, as well."

When I had the time, I wrote articles on how women —single *and* married—should secure their homes. My latest was aimed at domestic-violence survivors, and helping them feel safe. I donated my time to Nightingale House, a local shelter that helped women leaving DV situations, and I installed locks for them, free of charge.

"We should start a podcast," Sabrina said.

I wrinkled my nose. "I don't have time to sit around recording stuff." I did my fair share of callouts for jobs, plus at night I had to stay on top of the business-side of the store.

"Fine, fine." Sabrina leaned against the counter and eyed my jeans. "Damn, I hate you for being tall, long, and gorgeous. You're going to look *way* too beautiful as my maid of honor." She waved a hand between us. "You're all tall, sleek, and dark-haired, and I'm...the opposite."

I had some distant Black Irish ancestor to thank for my pale skin and ink-black hair. Growing up, I wanted to be short, blonde, and tanned. I snorted. "Beauty comes in all different forms, Sabrina." I gripped her shoulders. "You are so damn pretty, and your fiancé happens to think you are the most beautiful woman in the world. Andrew is gaga over you."

Sabrina sighed happily. "He does and he is." A pause. "So, do you have a date for my wedding yet?" My bestie's voice turned breezy and casual.

Uh-oh. I froze. All the wedding prep had sent my normally easygoing best friend a bit crazy. And I knew very well not to trust that tone.

I edged toward my office. "Not yet."

Sabrina's blue eyes sparked. "It's only *four* weeks away, Monroe. The maid of honor can't come alone."

"I'll be busy helping you out—"

"Find a date, Monroe."

"I don't want to just pick anyone for your wedding—"

Sabrina stomped her foot. "Find someone, or I'll find someone for you."

I held up my hands. "Okay, okay." I headed for my office. "I'll—" My cell phone rang. *Yes.* "I've got a call. Got to go." I dove through the office door.

"I won't forget," Sabrina yelled. "I'll revoke your best-friend status, if I have to."

I closed the door on my bridezilla bestie and looked at the phone.

Maguire. Finally.

I stabbed the call button. "Where have you been?"

"We have your brother," a robotic voice said.

My blood ran cold. My chest felt like it had filled with concrete.

"If you want to keep him alive, you'll do exactly as I say."

Zane

God, this party was boring.

Zane Roth sipped his wine and glanced around the ballroom at the Mandarin Oriental. The party held the Who's Who of New York society, all dressed up in their glittering best. The ceiling shimmered with a sea of crystal lights, tall flower arrangements dominated the tables, and the wall of windows had a great view of the Manhattan skyline.

Everything was picture perfect...and boring.

If it wasn't for the charity auction, he wouldn't be dressed in his tuxedo and dodging annoying people.

"I'm so sick of these parties," he muttered.

A snort came from beside him.

One of his best friends, Maverick Rivera, sipped his wine. "You were voted New York's sexiest billionaire bachelor. You should be loving this shindig."

Mav had been one of his best friends since college. Like Zane, Maverick hadn't come from wealth. They'd both earned it the old-fashioned way. Zane loved numbers and money, and had made Wall Street his hunting ground. Mav was a geek, despite not looking like a stereotypical one. He'd grown up in a strong, Mexican-American family, and with his brown skin, broad shoulders, and the fact that he worked out a lot, no one would pick him for a tech billionaire.

But under the big body, the man was a computer geek to the bone.

"All the society mamas are giving you lots of speculative looks." Mav gave him a small grin.

"Shut it, Rivera."

"They're all dreaming of marrying their daughters off to billionaire Zane Roth, the finance King of Wall Street."

Zane glared. "You done?"

"Oh, I could go on."

"I seem to recall another article about the billionaire bachelors. All three of us." Zane tipped his glass at his friend. "They'll be coming for you, next."

Mav's smile dissolved, and he shrugged a broad shoulder. "I'll toss Kensington at them. He's pretty."

Liam Kensington was the third member of their trio. Unlike Zane and Mav, Liam had come from money, although he worked hard to avoid his bloodsucking family.

Zane saw a woman in a slinky, blue dress shoot him a welcoming smile.

He looked away.

When he'd made his first billion, he'd welcomed the attention. Especially the female attention. He'd bedded more than his fair share of gorgeous women.

Of late, nothing and no one caught his interest. Women all left him feeling numb.

Work. He thrived on that.

A part of him figured he'd never find a woman who made him feel the same way as his work.

"Speak of the devil," Mav said.

Zane looked up to see Liam Kensington striding toward them. With the lean body of a swimmer, clad in a perfectly tailored tuxedo, he looked every inch the billionaire. His gold hair complemented a face the ladies oohed over.

People tried to get his attention, but the real estate mogul ignored everyone.

He reached Zane and Mav, grabbed Zane's wine, and emptied it in two gulps.

"I hate this party. When can we leave?" Having spent his formative years in London, he had a posh British accent. Another thing the ladies loved. "I have a contract to work on, my fundraiser ball to plan, and things to catch up on after our trip to San Francisco."

The three of them had just returned from a business trip to the West Coast.

"Can't leave until the auction's done," Zane said.

Liam sighed. His handsome face often had him voted the best-looking billionaire bachelor.

"Buy up big," Zane said. "Proceeds go to the Boys and Girls Clubs."

"One of your pet charities," Liam said.

"Yeah." Zane's father had left when he was seven. His mom had worked hard to support them. She was his hero. He liked to give back to charities that supported kids growing up in tough circumstances.

He'd set his mom up in a gorgeous house Upstate that she loved. And he was here for her tonight.

"Don't bid on the Phillips-Morley necklace, though," he added. "It's mine."

The necklace had a huge, rectangular sapphire pendant surrounded by diamonds. It was the real-life necklace said to have inspired the necklace in the movie, *Titanic*. It had been given to a young woman, Kate Florence Phillips, by her lover, Henry Samuel Morley. The two had run away together and booked passage on the Titanic.

Unfortunately for poor Kate, Henry had drowned when the ship had sunk. She'd returned to England with the necklace and a baby in her belly.

Zane's mother had always loved the story and pored over pictures of the necklace. She'd told him the story of the lovers, over and over.

"It was a gift from a man to a woman he loved. She was a shop girl, and he owned the store, but they fell in love, even though society frowned on their love." She sighed. "That's true love, Zane. Devotion, loyalty, through the good times and the bad."

Everything Carol Roth had never known.

Of course, it turned out old Henry was much older than his lover, and already married. But Zane didn't want to ruin the fairy tale for his mom.

Now, the Phillips-Morley necklace had turned up, and was being offered at auction. And Zane was going to get it for his mom. It was her birthday in a few months.

"Hey, is your fancy, new safe ready yet?" Zane asked Mav.

His friend nodded. "You're getting one of the first ones. I can have my team install it this week."

"Perfect." Mav's new Riv3000 was the latest in high-tech safes and said to be unbreakable. "I'll keep the necklace in it until my mom's birthday."

Someone called out Liam's name. With a sigh, their friend forced a smile. "Can't dodge this one. Simpson's an investor in my Brooklyn project. I'll be back."

"Need a refill?" Zane asked Mav.

"Sure."

Zane headed for the bar. He'd almost reached it when a manicured hand snagged his arm.

"Zane."

He looked down at the woman and barely swallowed his groan. "Allegra. You look lovely this evening."

She did. Allegra Montgomery's shimmery, silver dress

hugged her slender figure, and her cloud of mahogany brown hair accented her beautiful face. As the only daughter of a wealthy New York family—her father was from *the* Montgomery family and her mother was a former Miss America—Allegra was well-bred and well-educated but also, as he'd discovered, spoiled and liked getting her way.

Her dark eyes bored into him. "I'm sorry things ended badly for us the other month. I was..." Her voice lowered, and she stroked his forearm. "I miss you. I was hoping we could catch up again."

Zane arched a brow. They'd dated for a few weeks, shared a few dinners, and some decent sex. But Allegra liked being the center of attention, complained that he worked too much, and had constantly hounded him to take her on vacation. Preferably on a private jet to Tahiti or the Maldives.

When she'd asked him if it would be too much for him to give her a credit card of her own, for monthly expenses, Zane had exited stage left.

"I don't think so, Allegra. We aren't...compatible."

Her full lips turned into a pout. "I thought we were *very* compatible."

He cleared his throat. "I heard you moved on. With Chip Huffington."

Allegra waved a hand. "Oh, that's nothing serious."

And Chip was only a millionaire. Allegra would see that as a step down. In fact, Zane felt like every time she looked at him, he could almost see little dollar signs in her eyes.

He dredged up a smile. "I wish you all the best, Allegra. Good evening." He sidestepped her and made a beeline for the bar.

"What can I get you?" the bartender asked.

Wine wasn't going to cut it. It would probably be frowned on to ask for an entire bottle of Scotch. "Two glasses of Scotch, please. On the rocks. Do you have Macallan?"

"No, sorry, sir. Will Glenfiddich do?"

"Sure."

"Ladies and gentlemen," a voice said over the loudspeaker. The lights lowered. "I hope you're ready to spend big for a wonderful cause."

Carrying the drinks, Zane hurried back to Mav and Liam. He handed Mav a glass.

"Let's do this," Mav grumbled. "And next time, I'll make a generous online donation so I don't have to come to the party."

"Drinks at my place after I get the necklace," Zane said. "I have a very good bottle of Macallan."

Mav stilled. "How good?"

"Macallan 25. Single malt."

"I'm there," Liam said.

Mav lifted his chin.

Ahead, Zane watched the evening's host lift a black cloth off a pedestal. He stared at the necklace, the sapphire glittering under the lights.

There it was.

The sapphire was a deep, rich blue. Just like all the photos his mother had shown him.

"Get that damn necklace, Roth, and let's get out of here," Mav said.

Zane nodded. He'd get the necklace for the one woman in his life who rarely asked for anything, then escape the rest of the bloodsuckers and hang with his friends.

Billionaire Heists
Stealing from Mr. Rich
Blackmailing Mr. Bossman
Hacking Mr. CEO

W ant more action-packed romance? Then check out the men of **Norcross Security**.

The only man who can keep her safe is her boss' gorgeous brother.

Museum curator Haven McKinney has sworn off men. All of them. Totally. She's recently escaped a bad ex and started a new life for herself in San Francisco. She *loves* her job at the Hutton Museum, likes her new boss, and has made best friends with his feisty sister. Haven's also desperately trying *not* to notice their brother: hotshot investigator Rhys Norcross. And she's *really* trying not to notice his muscular body, sexy tattoos, and charming smile.

Nope, Rhys is off limits. But then Haven finds herself in the middle of a deadly situation...

Investigator Rhys Norcross is good at finding his targets. After leaving an elite Ghost Ops military team, the former Delta Force soldier thrives on his job at his brother's security firm, Norcross Security. He's had his eye on smart, sexy Haven for a while, but the pretty curator with her eyes full of secrets is proving far harder to chase down than he anticipated.

Luckily, Rhys never, ever gives up.

When thieves target the museum and steal a multi-million-dollar painting in a daring theft, Haven finds herself in trouble, and dangers from her past rising. Rhys vows to do whatever it takes to keep her safe, and Haven finds herself risking the one thing she was trying so hard to protect—her heart.

Norcross Security
The Investigator
The Troubleshooter
The Specialist
The Bodyguard
The Hacker

The Powerbroker
The Detective
The Medic
The Protector
Also Available as Audiobooks!

ALSO BY ANNA HACKETT

Sentinel Security

Wolf

Hades

Also Available as Audiobooks!

Norcross Security

The Investigator

The Troubleshooter

The Specialist

The Bodyguard

The Hacker

The Powerbroker

The Detective

The Medic

The Protector

Also Available as Audiobooks!

Billionaire Heists

Stealing from Mr. Rich

Blackmailing Mr. Bossman

Hacking Mr. CEO

Also Available as Audiobooks!

Team 52

Mission: Her Protection

Mission: Her Rescue

Mission: Her Security

Mission: Her Defense

Mission: Her Safety

Mission: Her Freedom

Mission: Her Shield

Mission: Her Justice

Also Available as Audiobooks!

Treasure Hunter Security

Undiscovered

Uncharted

Unexplored

Unfathomed

Untraveled

Unmapped

Unidentified

Undetected

Also Available as Audiobooks!

Galactic Kings

Overlord

Emperor

Captain of the Guard

Conqueror

Also Available as Audiobooks!

Eon Warriors

Edge of Eon

Touch of Eon

Heart of Eon

Kiss of Eon

Mark of Eon

Claim of Eon

Storm of Eon

Soul of Eon

King of Eon

Also Available as Audiobooks!

Galactic Gladiators: House of Rone

Sentinel

Defender

Centurion

Paladin

Guard

Weapons Master

Also Available as Audiobooks!

Galactic Gladiators

Gladiator

Warrior

Hero

Protector

Champion

Barbarian

Beast

Rogue

Guardian

Cyborg

Imperator

Hunter

Also Available as Audiobooks!

Hell Squad

Marcus

Cruz

Gabe

Reed

Roth

Noah

Shaw

Holmes

Niko

Finn

Devlin

Theron

Hemi

Ash

Levi

Manu

Griff

Dom

Survivors

Tane

Also Available as Audiobooks!

The Anomaly Series

Time Thief

Mind Raider

Soul Stealer

Salvation

Anomaly Series Box Set

The Phoenix Adventures

Among Galactic Ruins

At Star's End

In the Devil's Nebula

On a Rogue Planet

Beneath a Trojan Moon

Beyond Galaxy's Edge

On a Cyborg Planet

Return to Dark Earth

On a Barbarian World

Lost in Barbarian Space

Through Uncharted Space

Crashed on an Ice World

Perma Series

Winter Fusion

A Galactic Holiday

Warriors of the Wind

Tempest

Storm & Seduction

Fury & Darkness

Standalone Titles

Savage Dragon

Hunter's Surrender

One Night with the Wolf

For more information visit www.annahackett.com

ABOUT THE AUTHOR

I'm a USA Today bestselling romance author who's passionate about ***fast-paced, emotion-filled*** contemporary romantic suspense and science fiction romance. I love writing about people overcoming unbeatable odds and achieving seemingly impossible goals. I like to believe it's possible for all of us to do the same.

I live in Australia with my own personal hero and two very busy, always-on-the-move sons.

For release dates, behind-the-scenes info, free books, and other fun stuff, sign up for the latest news here:

Website: www.annahackett.com

Made in the USA
Columbia, SC
20 December 2022

74640887R00167